D1392180

The students at Corpus Christi Primary School,
Brixton, south London
The coolest Agatha fans anywhere

1.

A CHANCE ENCOUNTER

'You've been gazing at that painting for at least ten minutes.'

Liam appears at my side, head tilted in front of Vincent Van Gogh's *Sunflowers*. It's a Tuesday in November, and we're in the National Gallery on a school trip. 'You'd think it had one of those hidden pictures in it, the way you've been staring at it,' he continues. 'You know – the sort you can only see if you look at it for long enough?'

'It's just my favourite, that's all,' I say, smiling at him.

'I can tell!'

'Mum loved it too. She used to bring me to see it whenever we were passing this way.'

'How many times have you visited this place, just to *behold its beauty*?' He says the last bit dramatically, sweeping his arm round with a flourish, as if he's reciting a very corny poem.

I laugh. 'Quite a lot!' Then I pause. 'It looks different today, though.'

'How do you mean?'

I point to the vase, where the name 'Vincent' appears in blue script. 'Well, that bit's the same shade as normal, but the flowers –' I gesture to the yellow petals – 'they're paler and *clearer*, if that makes sense.'

'Less orangey-brown?' suggests Liam.

'Exactly!' I smile at him. Nobody gets me like Liam.

Liam shrugs. 'Perhaps they've had it cleaned.'

'That would make sense . . . although I was actually wondering if it was more to do with where it's hanging now. I mean, they've moved it from its usual spot, to make it part of the Van Gogh exhibition, so maybe the lighting's different.'

My friend Brianna arrives at my other side. Her

hair is still a sedate brown rather than her preferred blue – Dr Hargrave, our headmaster, has told her she mustn't dye it an 'unnatural' colour again – only now it's shaved everywhere except on top. She has delicate features and the contrast is almost shocking. Weirdly, though, it's a good look for her.

'Is it time to go home yet?' she asks, studying her nails. They're black with pale-green skulls.

'Don't think so,' says Liam. 'We've only seen one room so far.'

My backpack's on the floor. Brianna crouches down and starts rummaging in the front pocket.

'Hey, what are you doing?' I ask.

'Looking for that ultraviolet torch thing. Did you bring it?'

'It should be in there,' I say. 'What do you need it for?'

'My nails are meant to glow,' she replies.

I fish in the pouch of my bag and pull out the little torch, which is the size of a pen. 'Here you go.'

'Thanks,' Brianna says. She shines it on her nails and we all admire the gleaming skulls.

'Er . . . please can I have everyone's attention for a moment?' We turn round as Mrs Shelley, our art teacher, is trying to make herself noticed. All her clothes are drab browns and greys, and even her hair is an indeterminate sort of browny grey. She's like a washed-out, watercolour version of a person. I find myself wondering what Agatha Christie's Poirot would have made of her if he'd met her. I imagine my favourite detective nodding wisely and saying, *'Non, mam'selle*, there is no such thing as a really calm sea,' in his Belgian accent. And maybe he'd have been right – perhaps Mrs Shelley does have hidden depths.

'Er . . . everyone . . .' she says again in her whisper of a voice, 'can we move on now, please?'

I glance round at the other students. They must have finished looking at the paintings some while ago, because they're all gathered round the benches and windows, chatting and chewing gum. One group of students are all busy doing each other's hair, while some others are sitting on the floor, sharing things on their phones and laughing loudly. No one is listening to Mrs Shelley.

Brianna's lost concentration again, and is aiming the torch at a landscape on a side wall. Then she points it at the next painting and starts moving the beam along, one picture at a time, until she rounds the corner and reaches *Sunflowers*. Until this one, the beam has been invisible, but now there's something that shouldn't be there. I move in closer.

'Look,' I say, pointing to a small mark that's appeared, just below Van Gogh's signature.

Liam frowns. 'It looks like an "A".'

'It *is* an "A", I say. 'But what's it doing there?' I take a picture of it, while it's lit by the ultraviolet beam. The letter is quite ornate.

'Maybe it's a mark made by the gallery . . . their way of marking against theft?' he suggests.

'You really think they'd write on a priceless painting?' I ask.

Brianna shrugs. 'It is in invisible ink.'

Suddenly there's a loud clapping and we all go

quiet, our heads swivelling towards the source of the noise. A tall, slender man with dark, greying hair, brown eyes and an expensive-looking navy suit is standing there. This is Lord Rathbone, father of Sarah, my archenemy at school. She's standing next to him, a smug smile doing nothing to improve her habitual air of privilege and arrogance.

Normally, I love visiting the National Gallery, and I'd been looking forward to the Van Gogh exhibition for months. But it turns out that Sarah's dad is a gallery patron and the fact that this trip had been arranged was entirely thanks to him, so all the pleasure's been squeezed out of it like water from a mop.

Lord Rathbone smiles at us and I wince unexpectedly. I have an unpleasant image of him catching small prey in that sinister grin. He's like one of those toothed Venus flytrap plants.

'Please do your teacher the courtesy of paying attention to her words of wisdom,' he says. 'We are, after all, here to learn.' His voice has the oily tone of someone who's used to getting his own way.

Brianna leans in to my ear. 'Ugh, he's even more patronising than his daughter,' she whispers.

I nod and murmur, 'At least now we know where she gets it from.'

'He gives me the creeps,' she replies.

'Me too,' I agree.

Mrs Shelley clears her throat and says . . . something.

'What's that, Mrs S?' asks a boy.

'I can't hear her,' says another. 'Can you?'

Liam leans in to my ear. 'She said it's time to move on to the next room.'

'How do you know?' I ask him.

'I've been learning lip-reading. I thought it might come in useful.'

Lord Rathbone claps his hands again and shouts, *'Silence!'* He's gone an impressive deep red, which I'd like to inspect more closely. I think it's shade #9A0000 in the hexadecimal code used to identify precise colours on computers, but it's hard to tell without getting nearer to him than would be polite.

'I will not tolerate this insolence!' he exclaims.

'You will listen to your teacher with respect!' Everyone falls silent and he nods to Mrs Shelley, who blushes.

'Er . . . right, thank you, Lord Rathbone. Now listen carefully, everyone. We're going to move on to the next room, where I'd like you to look out for the painting we studied in class, *Bedroom in Arles*, which was, of course, one of Van Gogh's own favourites. Remember what we discussed – the flattened perspective and the lack of shadows, and try to compare the style with the Japanese prints we looked at, and which the artist used for inspiration. Decide how successful you think he was. And don't forget to take notes, for discussion in class next time.'

We all traipse dutifully through to the next part of the exhibition. Brianna, Liam and I walk along together, and Brianna asks, 'What did she say? Something about a Japanese prince?'

Liam laughs. 'Don't you remember those prints we looked at, to see how Van Gogh tried to get a similar effect in his work?'

She shakes her head. 'I don't really listen in art. I mean, I like looking at the pictures and stuff, but Mrs S is so dull that I always end up switching off.'

'Did you know she's actually a lady?' I ask her.

'Well, I didn't think she was a bloke, did I?'

'Agatha means as in "her ladyship",' says Liam.

'Seriously?' says Brianna. 'She's not half as arrogant as the Rathbones, though, is she?'

Liam laughs again. 'No one's half as arrogant as the Rathbones.'

'Shh!' I warn them. Sarah and her dad keep walking past, like guards on patrol.

We can't get near *Bedroom in Arles*, so we stand chatting at the back of the crowd. But after six or seven minutes staring at the back of people's heads, I grow restless.

'I'm going to have another look at *Sunflowers*,' I tell my friends. 'I can't work out what that letter A's doing on there. Can you cover for me?'

'How are we expected to do that?' asks Brianna.

'Say I've gone to the loo?' I suggest, then as soon

as I see the Rathbones chatting to our art teacher, I sneak out and return to the previous room, which is now empty. Except it's not quite empty – there's a boy standing in front of *Sunflowers*. He glances up as I approach.

'I love this work,' he says in a familiar way, as if we're friends.

'Mmm, me too,' I say.

'I always look at *Sunflowers* when I come to the gallery.'

'Mmm, me too!' *I really must think of something else to say.* 'It's one of my favourites,' I add, and my gaze flickers over him, taking in details:

HAIR: BLOND, WITH A LONG FRINGE
THAT SEEMS TO IRRITATE HIM –
HE KEEPS TOSSING HIS HEAD

Eyes: green, with brown flecks
(shade 8 according to the chart
on my bedroom wall)

Clothes: smart casual – a plain black winter coat over indigo jeans and a black sweater

Age: 16? 17? No sign of beard growth, but he might have shaved before coming out

HEIGHT: ABOUT FIVE FOOT SEVEN OR EIGHT

Build: slight, yet toned – he works out

I realise he's watching me with a smile, and I feel myself blush.

'So, you're a fan of Van Gogh too?' I say, changing the subject.

'I'm a fan of art in general,' he says. 'I've studied it for years. Did you know that there were two series of sunflowers, painted by Vincent for his friend and fellow artist Paul Gauguin? He was going to hang them as a frieze round the walls of Gauguin's room in the Yellow House in Arles.'

Actually, I *do* know that, but before I get a chance to respond, the boy is walking over to the next painting along: *Wheatfield with Cypresses.*

'Look at the impasto!' he exclaims.

I know that this means having several coats of paint layered one on top of another, to build texture, so I can at least nod. Van Gogh is said to have been one of the first painters to use the technique.

'You can really feel the movement of the trees and clouds, can't you?' he asks.

'You really can,' I say, excited to find someone who shares my love of Van Gogh's art. I've never met anyone else who's known what 'impasto' means. 'I've been having to keep my hands behind my back, so I don't touch the surface. It's so tempting.'

He glances round, one hand hovering just in front of the painting's surface. 'Shall we?'

'*No!*' I cry.

He bursts out laughing. 'I wouldn't really. It might be brittle, after all these years – I don't want to be the boy who breaks one of Van Gogh's masterpieces. I'm Arthur, by the way.'

'Like Hercule Poirot's friend!' I say. I can't stop myself blurting it out.

He smiles and bows. 'Captain Arthur Hastings, at your service.'

'You know the books?' I say excitedly.

'Know them? I've led my life according to the belief system of Hercule Poirot. I like to pretend my parents named me after his friend – but it was actually after some boring great-uncle or other.'

'Well, I can do one better than that.' I grin. 'I'm named after the author herself,' I announce. 'I'm Agatha.' We beam at each other. 'So . . . do you work here?' I finally ask.

'I wish! No – I'm doing work experience at a printer's nearby. I come in on my lunch hour, or if it's quiet and there's nothing for me to do at work. I'm not allowed to operate the machinery or anything, so when they're busy I just get out from under their feet.' He shakes his head in wonder, staring at *Wheatfield with Cypresses*. 'Just look at that craftsmanship. It's exquisite.'

'It really is,' I say. We stand side by side in silence for a moment. There's something awe-inspiring about getting as close as this to a famous painting.

'Well, I guess I'd better get back to the others,' I say eventually.

He nods. 'And they might have started to miss me at the printer's. I'm not really supposed to go wandering off.'

We wave goodbye to each other and I walk quietly back through to the next room. Although it was great meeting Arthur, I wish I'd had another chance to look at that letter A. It reminds me of the first of the three tests I'd had to complete to become an agent – I only had an A to start with then as well. There's no one in this part of the exhibition, so I spend a moment in front of another of my favourites, *The Starry Night*, with its yellow moon and swirly sky. Then I do my duty and examine *Bedroom in Arles* – admiring the bright colours and the bold simplicity of the bed, chair and door. I remember learning that the walls and door were originally purple rather than their current shade of blue: the paint has discoloured a lot over the years. The painting hangs beside *The Yellow House* – a picture of the house in Arles in which the bedroom was situated. Finally, I creep through to the next area, where Mrs Shelley is with the other students.

'There you are!' hisses Brianna. 'You've been gone for ages! Mrs S asked where you were, and we had to say you'd got diarrhoea.'

'Diarrhoea?' I say in horror. Then I take in the glint in her eye. She's just joking. She laughs.

'Actually,' says Liam, pushing his glasses up his nose, 'nobody even noticed.'

'Just another day of invisibility,' I say brightly.

'Do you really want this lot to notice you?' says Brianna.

She has a point. There's quite a lot of rivalry at St Regis. Lots of students live extraordinarily privileged lives, from a financial point of view at least. Their families own estates – or even whole islands. I attend the school on a scholarship and live in a park cottage, because my dad's the head gardener there. I guess that's still pretty privileged, but not by their standards. I wouldn't change places with them for anything, though.

We take the minibuses back to school. Liam, Brianna and I sit close together, and I tell them about meeting Arthur.

'Tall, blond and pretentious?' says Liam. 'Are you sure he's not a St Regis boy?'

I roll my eyes. 'He was *nice*, Liam. And not at all pretentious – he just knows stuff, that's all.'

'Whatever,' he says.

Brianna starts singing some rhyme or other about Liam being jealous because he loves me and wants to do 'kissing in a tree'. We ignore her. We learnt long ago that it's the only way to get her to stop – she quickly gets bored if she can't provoke a reaction.

We get back to St Regis just in time to take the register and then it's time to head home.

'Why does the school always insist we come back here after a trip?' complains Brianna. Then she waves goodbye and walks over to a red sports car – her brother's. He's revving the engine, as if he can't wait a moment longer. He's one of those impatient, unreliable types and frequently lets Brianna down. But, as her parents are rarely in the country, he's pretty much all she's got.

I walk with Liam to his bus stop. I'm wearing my beautiful red wool coat (a birthday present from my dad), and my matching beret to keep my head warm, but there's a cold wind that makes my ears ache. I pull my hat down as far as it will go and stuff my gloved hands in my pockets. It's already dark and the streetlights cast orange reflections in the puddles.

'Any word from the Gatekeepers?' Liam asks as we walk.

'Only the homework they keep giving me – no sign of an actual case,' I reply.

The Gatekeepers' Guild is the secret crime-fighting organisation that I'm an agent for. I'm their newest and youngest recruit – Agent Cipher X (OK – I made up the code name, but maybe it will catch on).

'I don't know why the professor said I'd be getting my first case soon,' I grumble. 'I haven't heard a thing from her or from Sofia.'

Professor D'Oliveira is high up in the Gatekeepers' organisation. She assigned the second-youngest Guild member, Sofia Solokov, to me as my mentor. The last four times when I've been over to HQ, there's just been a folder full of homework waiting for me – ciphers to solve or information on new Guild rules and policies (as if the 3,051-page rule book wasn't already enough).

We reach his bus stop and he waits in the shelter, rubbing his arms for warmth. I can see the steam from his breath in the bus-stop lighting.

'I'm sure you'll hear soon,' he says. 'After all, they were clearly impressed by your work on the museum murder and the water poisoning.'

'I guess,' I say with a shrug. 'But sometimes I worry they're going to forget about me.'

'Forget about *you*? Agatha Oddlow, crime-fighter extraordinaire?' he says in mock horror. 'Never!'

I laugh. Liam's always so good at cheering me up.

'Anyway,' he continues, 'since when have you waited to be *allocated* an investigation?'

'True . . . Maybe I should go over to headquarters,' I say, 'and ask for a case. It might just be that the professor is waiting for me to be proactive.'

Liam nods. 'I think that's a good plan. And if all else fails, we could always investigate that woman over there,' he says, pointing to a middle-aged woman across the street, who's rummaging in a plastic bag. 'She looks very suspicious.' As he says this, the woman draws out a banana, peels it and takes a bite. 'Definitely sinister,' he says. 'Could this be one for the Oddlow Agency?' He raises an eyebrow.

I laugh. We've neglected our detective agency since I became a real investigator. The Oddlow Agency ('No Case Too Odd' – its motto inspired by my surname) seems a bit like a game now – almost as if we were different people back then. It feels as though we've done a lot of growing up in a short space of time.

Liam's bus approaches, and he holds out his arm to signal to the driver to stop. It pulls up and Liam climbs aboard. I wave through the window at his outline, which is strangely distorted by the glass, then I continue along my way. I'll drop off my school bag at home and change into more practical clothes, before heading over to the Guild headquarters.

It's not far to get home to Hyde Park, and I walk quickly. The embassies are all lit up as I pass. When I reach the park, there aren't many people around. All the dog-walkers have their collars turned up and woolly hats pulled down low, exposing as little skin as possible to the cold wind lifting off the Serpentine lake. Even their dogs look subdued.

When I open the door to Groundskeeper's Cottage and step inside, our cat comes running up to meet me, winding himself tightly round my legs and knocking me off balance.

I laugh as I try to right myself.

'Hey, Oliver, boy! Did you miss me?'

'Meow!'

'What you're really missing is dinner, aren't you?' I check my watch. It's only four thirty. 'It's a bit early, though, isn't it?'

Oliver's unimpressed when I open the door to the

staircase and run up to my bedroom. I can hear him wailing at me from the bottom of the stairs. 'Sorry!' I call down. 'You'll get fat if you start eating between meals.'

It takes me five minutes to change out of my uniform and into black jeans, a black sweater and my Doc Martens boots. After a moment's hesitation, I put on a navy waterproof jacket with a hood. Not my style, but needs must – the tunnel I have to pass through will be dirty and damp. Another five minutes and I've assembled a powerful head torch, gloves and my notebook and pen to go in my backpack along with my martial arts outfit. My Guild key is always round my neck, so I'm sorted. The key is my favourite possession. It belonged to my mother when she was a Guild agent – and it opens entrances to underground tunnels all over London.

Downstairs, I scribble a note to Dad, in case he finishes early:

Gone jogging.
Back by 6.

I use a magnet to fix the message to the fridge, while Oliver winds himself round my ankles, meowing to be fed. At last, I take pity on him (after all, he was Mum's cat, and I'm weak where he's concerned) and spoon a small portion of food into his bowl.

'Stinky fish for you,' I tell him, as I plonk the dish on the floor. Then I leave the house and head over to the locked grille beside the Serpentine – at a jog, so my message to Dad won't be a lie.

It's time to head underground.

2.

THE BEGINNING

Unlocking the grille with my key, I slip inside. The smell that hits me is like seaweed mixed with rotten cabbage – but it's still far better than when the polluted algae had taken over. Fitting my head torch, I switch it on, and the bright LED beam illuminates the gloomy, uneven space. I hate this passage to the network of tunnels that run under much of London, but it's my nearest entrance. The low headroom means I have to stay at a crouch throughout. At least experience has taught me to protect my hands with gloves, and to free them up by using the head torch.

I shuffle along as quickly as I can to get through the narrow corridor to the cave at the end. But being in darkness always makes a difficult journey seem slower and I'm soon feeling as though I'll never get out of this place. I have to stop a couple of times to rub my cramping calves. When I do, the reality of where I am crowds in on me – deep underground, and no one knows I'm here – and I have to slow my breathing and focus on my destination.

At last, I see the passage open out ahead, so I speed up. Reaching the cavern, I stretch and groan, easing out my neck and legs. Then I walk over to the brick wall, where the familiar big cast-iron door is almost fully camouflaged. It opens readily with my key and I step through on to the welcome mat that protects a plush red carpet. I'm inside the headquarters of the Gatekeepers' Guild.

Professor D'Oliveira's office is one of many down a long corridor. Along the way, I pass doors bearing other staff members' names and it occurs to me – not for the first time – how many people are involved in the organisation. I haven't even met most of these agents and administrative staff, yet they're clearly an integral part of the Guild. I start to feel quite small by comparison – and I'm not comfortable with the feeling.

At the door marked PROFESSOR D. D'OLIVEIRA, I knock and she gives a brisk 'Enter!'

Inside, the 'little old lady' (her own words, which really don't do her justice) looks up from a document on her desk and raises her eyebrows.

'Agatha? I wasn't expecting you today . . .?' Her Caribbean accent is slightly stronger when she's surprised – it's the only 'tell' she has – the only clue to her real emotions.

I shake my head. 'I know,' I say, 'but I was hoping to talk to you.' It's strange how much less confident I feel, now that I'm faced with the professor. She has a big presence for such a small, neat person, and it's hard not to be . . . intimidated.

'Have a seat.' She gestures to one of the curved wooden chairs in front of her desk, and I sit down.

'Thank you – I was just . . .' I hesitate.

'You were just wondering when we were going to

give you that much-anticipated first case?' she suggests.

I nod. 'I just . . . I feel . . .' I take a deep breath: 'I've saved London twice now but you haven't trusted me with a case of my own yet.' It sounds slightly childish, but at least I've said it.

She surveys me. I can't read her expression, and I look down at my hands. My purple nail varnish needs a retouch. At last, she sits back in her green leather chair and folds her hands in her lap.

'You are very young, Agatha . . .'

'But I'm more than capable!'

She holds up a hand. 'Please don't interrupt. What I was about to say was that, despite your youth and relative inexperience, it has been suggested to me that you might be able to help out with a case I've received. We're short of available agents at the moment.'

Please, please don't say I've ruined it by whining like a spoilt brat . . .

'Really?' I say, holding my breath.

She nods. 'I would have placed Sofia Solokov on

this investigation, but another agent is on sick leave, so Sofia's had to take over their cases and won't have time to start on this one.' She checks her watch. 'Your new partner is not currently in the building. Please come in at nine thirty tomorrow morning and I'll introduce you.'

New partner? I'm so shocked, I have to blink back tears. 'My . . . partner?' I stammer. 'I didn't realise I'd have to work with someone else . . .'

'That is what I meant, when I said that you're still very young, inexperienced. It will be beneficial to your skillset for you to learn to work as part of a team.'

I flush. 'Oh, right. Yes, I see . . .' I move to stand up. Then I remember my mum – an agent in the Guild herself. I know she didn't die when her bike collided with a car, which is what the police told Dad and me seven years ago. 'Professor?'

She's already gone back to reading a document. 'Hmm?'

'Have you heard any more . . . about who took my mum's file?'

She looks up. 'No, Agatha, I'm afraid not. I was really hoping we'd have some answers by now. It troubles me to think of the Guild as vulnerable in this way – that a file could go missing. I hate having to mistrust so many people—' She stops abruptly, as if she's giving too much away. 'But I do have some of my most trusted agents working on finding your mother's missing file and, I promise you, as soon as we have any information, you'll be among the first to hear about it.'

'Thank you,' I say. 'Goodbye, Professor.'

'Goodbye, Agatha. See you tomorrow, at nine thirty.'

'Yes, see you then.'

Heading out of the area housing the offices, I reach the main corridor. From here, I can proceed to any part of London. I check my watch. It's only quarter to five. I didn't make it to kung fu training yesterday, so I decide to head to the *dojo* – the gym where I learn with my *sifu* (master teacher), Mr Zhang.

It's not far to Soho from here, so I set off, jogging along the tunnels as both a warm-up and a continuation of my promise to Dad. As I run, I think back to the day I was accepted into the Guild – and then the discovery that my mum's dossier was missing from the file rooms. I'd spent so much time believing that, when I found out who or what she'd been investigating, I'd finally have some answers, but without the file all that information was gone . . .

I wipe away an angry tear as I think about it again and focus on my breathing, drawing strength from the pumping of my lungs and heart. *I will find out. I will find out*, I think, in time to the pounding of my feet.

Back above ground, Mr Zhang's granddaughter greets me at the door of the Black Bamboo restaurant.

'Agatha, hi!'

'Hi, Bai! Is your grandfather busy? I was hoping to train.'

'He's downstairs. Do you have your *gi*?' She's referring to my white training tunic and trousers.

I hold up my backpack. 'Always.'

I change in a tiny room at the back, leaving my clothes neatly folded on a chair. There's a framed Chinese symbol on the wall that represents the name for a dish called biang biang noodles. I study it for a moment. It's famous for being hard to write, and even my near-photographic brain has trouble remembering every ink mark.

'*Sifu*.'

We bow to one another, then Mr Zhang nods and says, 'Show me the new sequence I taught you.'

I work through it, concentrating hard as I turn, kicking and punching the air and keeping my weight low to the ground.

'Good,' he says. 'Very good. You are making excellent progress. We will make a master of you yet.'

'Thank you, *sifu*,' I say, bowing my head.

He has me work on various moves and then use a punch bag.

'Focus!' he shouts. 'When your mind is distracted, you lose the essential balance of mind and body.'

'Yes, *sifu*.'

We work until I'm out of breath. I check my watch. It's half past five. I need to hurry if I'm to keep my promise to be back at the cottage by six. I thank Mr Zhang, run upstairs to get changed and shout my goodbyes to him and Bai.

I jog all the way home. It's amazing how much fitter I am now that I train regularly. The route is lovely – the whole of Oxford Street is lit up with early-Christmas windows, and it's hard not to keep stopping to admire the scenes.

Balance and focus, I remind myself, thinking of my lesson with Mr Zhang.

I can't help wondering who my partner in the Guild will be. What if they're like Sofia – bossy and judgemental?

Back home, I follow a trail of muddy items through the hallway – boots, fleece and gardening gloves –

until I find Dad in the kitchen, making dinner. Oliver greets me again, purring loudly as he rubs against my legs.

'Hi, Dad!'

'Hi, Aggie. How was the jog?'

'Bracing!' I shiver. 'Were you OK working outside today?'

'Oh, you know me – I don't mind the cold. We retreated to the glasshouses once it got dark. Omelettes OK again?'

'Great. Do you want me to make them?' I offer.

'No, I've got it. You go for your shower.'

'OK! Then shall I make a fire in the living room?'

'Good plan,' he says. 'Let's eat in there – it'll be nice and cosy.'

After my wash, Oliver comes with me to the living room and keeps me company as I set to work building a fire in the little stove. Dad's taught me how to do this, using old newspaper as kindling and waiting for the flame to catch. It's important to keep the stove door open at this stage. Then, when it's blazing, I add pieces of wood – but not large ones nor too many, or the fire will be suffocated. Once it's burning reliably, the door can be shut.

'There,' I tell Oliver, as I take a seat on the sofa and spread a fleecy throw over my legs. 'That's better, isn't it?'

His purring reaches new decibels and he leaps on to my lap, where he turns round several times before deciding on the optimal position and curling up. His whole body starts to vibrate with contentment. I've read that stroking a pet can lower a person's heart rate and blood pressure. I'm probably a bit too young to worry about either of those, but there's definitely something soothing about running my hands over Oliver's smooth fur.

Dad brings in dinner and I eat carefully, holding my plate up close to my chin, so I don't drop any hot food on the cat. My omelette is filled with Cheddar cheese and baked beans – my favourite combination.

'So, how was the trip?' he asks.

'Interesting, thanks.'

He raises an eyebrow. 'I thought you found your art teacher – Mrs Sheldon . . . Shelby . . .? – boring?'

'Shelley.'

'As in the poet?'

'Yep. And she is boring. But the paintings were amazing, and there was this boy there, who knew all about art.'

'What? Surely not more than you?'

'Maybe a little bit . . .' I grin. 'It was weird, though – the *Sunflowers* painting had been moved for the Van Gogh exhibition and it looked different in its new spot.'

Dad takes a sip of water. 'Different how?'

'Paler . . . or brighter.' I sigh. 'Hard to explain – but Arthur didn't say anything about the change.'

'Arthur? Is that the young man?'

I nod. 'He loves that painting too. It's really interesting how just moving a picture to a different spot can change its appearance like that, isn't it?' Dad is nodding, listening intently. 'So . . . how are the cuttings?' I ask.

'They're coming along beautifully, thanks. We were potting up the yew today – it's getting quite bushy.'

'Yew,' I say, closing my eyes and consulting my internal filing system. '*Taxus Baccata. Widely planted in churchyards, to keep it away from livestock, because of its toxicity.*'

'Very good. Although there is a lot of interesting debate these days as to the motives for churchyard planting . . .'

I zone out. It's a terrible habit, but I just can't focus on Dad's horticulture lectures. My mind keeps skipping ahead to tomorrow morning, when I'll find out who my partner's going to be. *They can't be worse than Sofia*, I reason. It's still nerve-wracking, though, to contemplate having to work with someone I don't know. It's not exactly how I'd pictured my first case.

'So, there you have it,' finishes Dad brightly. 'The debate around the common yew.'

'Great, Dad.' I finish scraping the last of the tomato sauce off my plate and put down my fork. 'Look, I have homework . . .'

I don't need to finish the sentence. 'Sure – I'll wash up,' he says. He puts on a bad French accent. 'After all, if ze little grey cells are not exercised, zey grow ze rust.'

'Are you misquoting Poirot at me?'

'Hey! Why should you get all the fun?' He has a point.

'Thank you for tea – and for washing up.' I stand up and give him a kiss on the cheek before heading up to my attic bedroom.

Sitting at my desk, staring at the maths sheet in front of me, I find the numbers beginning to blur. I swivel in my chair and my eyes alight on the pile of red notebooks on a high shelf. These contain all the information I've collated over the years about my mum's death. I don't believe she was killed in a bicycle accident, but I still don't know what did happen to her. I seem to be thwarted every time I try to find out.

You see, Mum – Clara Oddlow – was an agent of the Gatekeepers' Guild before I'd even heard of it. By becoming an agent myself, I'd planned to gain access to her files, to find out what she was working on when she died.

My mind drifts back to that day in the summer, when Professor D'Oliveira and Sofia had taken me to the Guild file rooms, but I found the folders bearing my mum's name had been emptied of documents and filled with blank paper.

I shake off these unhappy memories and focus on the maths questions I've been set as homework. I'm pretty good at maths, but nothing compared to Liam. Still, it doesn't take me long to get the work done. I sigh with satisfaction as I slip my exercise book back into my backpack.

I get up from the chair and lie down on my bed. It's cold and draughty, so I snuggle under the duvet. From here, I can see all the charts and artefacts that mark this room as mine. There's the map of London, the bust of Queen Victoria, the beautiful hardback editions of Agatha Christie's crime novels and her short stories. There are also the two clothes racks with my assortment of outfits and costumes, some of which have been useful for disguising myself during cases.

As I change for bed, I glance over at the photo beside my bed. It's of my mum astride her bike, one foot on the ground for balance.

'I will find out what happened to you, Mum – I promise,' I tell her for the thousandth time. But I mean it – I won't rest until I have all the answers. Before I go to sleep, I tell her about Arthur, and his fascination with the impasto texture of Van Gogh's painting. It was good to meet someone who shares my passion for beautiful things and didn't think me odd for being obsessed with *Sunflowers*.

'Night, Mum,' I tell her, as I turn off the light.

3.

INTRODUCTIONS

I leap out of bed when my alarm goes off on Wednesday morning. My dreams have been filled with images of potential partners, from a very frail old man to a supremely bossy Hermione Granger, and even an Inspector Gadget. It takes a while for my sleep-fogged brain to realise they aren't real.

Sliding my feet into my granddad-style tartan slippers and donning my dressing gown, I head downstairs.

Dad's up already, urgently shovelling cereal into his mouth, as if it's been several days since his last meal.

'Morning,' he says brightly through a mouthful of cornflakes.

'Morning.' I sit down at the table and reach for the Coco Pops.

'What's your schedule for today?' he teases.

'Oh, thought I'd go to school . . .'

'Mmm, why not?' He plays along. 'And maybe try not to run off and solve any mysteries?'

'Well, unless something comes up . . .'

He shakes his head. 'A hopeless case,' he says – but he's smiling.

I finish my cereal and run upstairs to clean my teeth and get changed into my uniform. I've worked out that I have time to show my face at registration, before finding a way to leave again. If I get marked as present this morning, I can keep my attendance figures from sinking too quickly. I add a floral scarf and my red beret, then pull on my coat. Having a sudden idea how to get out of school, I rummage through my disguises and add some items to my backpack.

Finally, I stuff another change of clothes as well

into my already bulging backpack – I have a feeling that school uniform would seriously undermine my credibility as an investigator.

Outside, the wind is still biting. I hurriedly fasten my coat right to the top and tighten the knot in my scarf. Then, despite my fatigue, I jog most of the way to school, keen to get out of the cold as quickly as possible. When I'm within sight of the school gates, I hear someone calling my name. Turning, I catch sight of Brianna. She's not hurrying – Brianna rarely rushes anywhere – and she looks almost blue with cold.

'Come on,' I say, 'I'm not staying out here any longer than I have to.'

One of the best things about St Regis is that we're allowed to go straight in when we arrive. As soon as we get inside, we find a radiator to lean against. Shivering, I glance around and catch sight of Liam, standing close by. He's talking to a girl I vaguely recognise from class. They seem to be discussing mathematical theories.

He grins at Brianna and me and says, 'Tamsin's also a fan of Fermat!'

'Is that the one with the salivating dogs?' asks Brianna.

'That's Pavlov,' Liam and I say in unison, and we both laugh.

'*Pierre de Fermat is considered one of the founders of the modern theory of numbers,*' I quote, from a piece I read the first time Liam mentioned Fermat, when I'd had no idea who he was. '*He was born in the early 1600s and was one of the leading mathematicians of the first half of the seventeenth century.*'

'Who needs Wikipedia when they've got Agatha?' says Brianna. She glances behind me and mutters, 'Incoming!'

We hold our breath as Sarah Rathbone and her entourage pass by. Sarah doesn't acknowledge us, thankfully, and we all breathe out with relief.

Without warning, a voice booms in my direction. 'Remove your coat, hat and scarf at once, Miss Oddlow! You're in school now!' It's our form teacher, the formidable Mrs Bodley-Finch, lurking in the corridor so she can jump out at unsuspecting students.

I'm convinced she has chameleon powers and can blend in to the background.

'Sorry, ma'am!' I take off the offending articles, folding the coat and scarf carefully and placing them all in my backpack. Liam and I call a 'See you later!' to Brianna and walk towards our form room.

'The professor's given me a case,' I whisper as we walk along. 'I'm going over to the Guild after the register.'

His eyes go wide. 'You went over there and asked her?'

I nod. 'And she said she had something for me.'

'That's great! So how will you get out of this place?'

'I've brought a disguise.'

Liam shakes his head and sighs. 'Aggie, no offence, but you did get caught when you tried to impersonate a health inspector. And a tree surgeon.'

'I know,' I say. 'That's why I've chosen a foolproof costume this time.'

We follow the other students into our form room, where I catch our teacher's eye and smile innocently.

'Morning, Mrs Bodley-Finch.'

She glowers and looks away. She has only two expressions: frowning and glowering. I wonder what it's like to be her husband, forever waiting for a smile that isn't going to come.

Liam and I take our usual seats in the middle of the room.

'What's your disguise?' he whispers.

But Mrs Bodley-Finch frowns at him and says, 'That's enough talking, Liam!'

As soon as we've escaped from registration, I head towards the girls' cloakroom to get changed. 'Let Brianna know what's going on, will you?' I murmur to Liam in parting.

'But wait,' he says, 'you haven't told me your disguise!' but I don't reply.

In the cloakroom, I pull my outfit from my backpack. I only have one school skirt, so after I've taken it off I'm careful to fold it neatly before placing it in my backpack with the rest of my uniform. I'm especially pleased with my disguise, which is the uniform for St Mary's School for Girls – the school just down the road from St Regis. I check in the mirror as I don my costume. With the addition of a blonde wig and blue-framed glasses, I'm unrecognisable. Better yet, I look uncannily like Meredith Atkins – this year's director of the St Mary's school play.

Let me explain. Every year, St Regis allows St Mary's School for Girls to use its state-of-the-art theatre for their school production – and St Mary's takes its annual production very seriously. I've seen Meredith coming and going, even in lesson times. She's only two years ahead of me, and I've envied her the ability to leave school at whim. Now, with wedge heels that raise me to around her height, I'm going to borrow her freedom.

When I reach reception, the secretary barely glances my way before pressing the button to open the door. I march out, arms round a folder that could easily conceal the script of a play (but actually holds my maths homework). The walk across the playground feels longer than ever before. It reminds me of those prison films, where there's a revolving light, picking out prisoners as they attempt to make a break for it. My heart's pounding at the thought that I could get caught just as I'm about to escape. But, just as I reach the metal gate, it swings open at the secretary's command, and I'm through! I take a deep breath of icy air and begin to walk, shivering without my coat.

At least I'll soon be underground.

Over the past few months, I've been introduced to a number of routes to the Guild HQ that are far more comfortable than the one beside the Serpentine. I choose one now – a well-built tunnel, which has its entrance right next to Grosvenor Square Gardens. There's a bike-hire rack close by, so I pay for a bicycle and wheel it over to the rhododendron bush, behind which the metal entrance door is sited.

Checking for onlookers, I dodge behind the large shrub and take my key from round my neck. It turns soundlessly in the well-oiled lock. I swing the door open, wheel the bike through and manage to close the door behind me. I've grown accustomed to bumping bicycles down steps into subterranean passageways. I use the torch on my phone to light my way to the bottom of the flight. Leaning my bike against the wall, I rummage in my backpack for yet another set of alternative clothes. It wouldn't be my first choice of changing room, but needs must. I don black trousers, a white shirt, a pair of smart trainers, and I pull my red coat out from the bottom of my bag, and I'm set to go. Then I mount the bike, push off and let its self-charging lamps illuminate the tunnels. I feel a bit as though I'm flying, with my coat billowing out behind me like a cape.

It takes less than ten minutes to reach the massive door that marks the main entrance to the Gatekeepers' Guild. Two armed guards check my pass and let me through. Leaving my hired bike in a set of racks provided for the purpose, I make my way through the various passages on foot, until I reach Professor D'Oliveira's office.

She calls 'Enter!' in answer to my knock, and I step inside. 'Good morning, Agatha. Please take a seat.'

She's sitting at her carved desk in her wood-panelled office, where everything is plush and ornate. The only clue that we're underground is the lack of windows.

I sit and she slides a folder across the desk towards me. 'Your first case for the Gatekeepers' Guild,' she says. As I reach to pick it up, there's another knock at the door . . . and who should enter but the boy from the National Gallery.

Arthur! My brain struggles to compute. There's a word, *incongruous*, which means something that looks completely out of place. This is not *his* territory, but mine. What on earth is he doing here?

'Ah!' says the professor. 'Arthur – thank you for joining us. Agatha, this is Arthur Fitzwilliam. Arthur, Agatha Oddlow. The two of you will be working on the case together.'

He grins sheepishly at me. 'Sorry – I looked on your school calendar and found out your class were visiting the gallery yesterday, so I couldn't resist popping in, in the hope we'd get a chance to meet.'

My brain feels foggy. 'But . . . you didn't say you had anything to do with the Guild!'

'Not really the place, was it?' he points out. 'I couldn't start blurting out about a top-secret organisation in public.'

The professor looks from me to Arthur and back. 'Have you two met already?' she asks, with a frown.

'Yes,' I say. 'Arthur faked a "chance encounter" with me at the National Gallery yesterday afternoon.'

'I see . . .' she says slowly. 'Arthur, please take a seat.'

As he sits, his face is full of happy mischief.

'Sorry, Professor D,' he says. But he's smiling.

'That was totally unprofessional conduct,' she says. 'It wasn't fair to Agatha – and it was in blatant breach of Guild rules.'

'Sorry, Professor,' he says again. 'But you told me I was going to be working with Agatha and—'

She holds up a hand to silence him – a gesture I've seen too many times directed at me. 'That will do.'

'But it's not like I told her anything!' he protests.

I can't help smiling. There was no malice in Arthur's actions, after all, and I *had* enjoyed meeting him. I reckon we'll have fun working together.

The professor shakes her head. 'I despair, I really do,' she says. But her eyes are twinkling and the corners of her mouth are twitching.

'So you knew we were going to be working together?' I say, turning to Arthur. 'When we met at the gallery, I mean.'

He nods. 'The professor told me yesterday morning.'

Professor D'Oliveira shakes her head. She turns to me. 'So, Agatha,' she says, 'you see what you have to deal with . . . Keep him on a tight leash, won't you?' But she's smiling indulgently, as if he's a favourite child.

'I will,' I promise.

'This is a sensitive investigation,' she says, looking from one of us to the other. 'But I'm sure you'll make an excellent team. Arthur, who has good art knowledge and more Guild experience, is the lead on this case, but I do expect you, Arthur, to listen to Agatha – she has good instincts and is a natural codebreaker. Right – I think that's everything for now. I need to get on with my own work.' She looks at Arthur. 'Take Agatha to the induction room and bring her up to speed with the case so far, would you?'

'Certainly, Professor,' he says. He picks up the folder and the pair of us stand up and move towards the door.

'Oh,' she says, 'just one more thing. Agatha, stay behind a moment, will you? We won't be long, Arthur.' Arthur nods and leaves the room, shutting the door behind him.

'Now, Agatha,' she says, 'don't let this young man take over completely. There's a case to be solved, and he needs a firm hand at times. He may have been an agent for a couple of years longer than you, but don't be afraid to contradict him, if you feel it's required.'

'OK,' I say. 'Thank you for trusting me with this.'

'You've already proven your worth, with the two cases you conducted outside of the Guild. Don't forget, though – it's not only Arthur who needs to toe the line. Now you're working for us, you can't be going off on your own. There are safeguarding issues at stake here – and I don't want to have to suspend you again.'

I feel myself flush with embarrassment and frustration. What do I have to do to make her trust me? 'I won't – I promise,' I say, biting back the urge to defend myself.

Arthur is waiting for me outside the office. He nods towards the corridor we need to take to the induction room, and we begin walking side by side. As we pass door after door, part of my mind marvels, as always, at the scale of this underground community.

'So, you're Clara Oddlow's daughter?' he says.

'How did you know that?' I ask.

He shrugs. 'Common knowledge within the Guild.'

'Oh.' I take that in. 'So, what do you know about her?'

'Well, she's a bit of a legend around here, isn't she? Something to live up to. Must be hard for you, as her daughter.'

'Well, if I let myself think too hard about it, I'd be

paralysed with fears of inadequacy and failure!' I laugh to show I'm not *entirely* serious.

'I believe it's best not to dwell on the negatives,' says Arthur. 'Life's hard enough at times, without setting yourself up to fail.'

'That's exactly what I think!' We smile at each other. 'What's the case?' I ask him. 'Professor D'Oliveira said you're an art expert, so I'm guessing it's about art?'

'It is indeed,' said Arthur. 'Let's go in here and then I'll fill you in.' He opens the door to the induction room. Unlike the previous times I've visited this space, now there are a number of other people sitting at tables, mainly sifting through files. We take seats on the far side, near the radiator. The cold wind doesn't reach these offices, but it's still distinctly chilly underground.

I glance around. One man is studying something that looks like a photo, but he's using his phone to examine it.

'What's he doing?' I whisper to Arthur.

'It's a special app. The thing he's examining is a bit like a microfiche – do you know about those?'

I squeeze my eyes shut for a moment as I summon up my mental filing cabinet and flick through the imaginary, hand-written cards until I reach the right one:

'A flat piece of film containing microphotographs of the pages of a document,' I say, reading the text inside my mind.

'That's right – tiny images, which you have to view through a special machine that magnifies them. Well, this is a thing called a nanofiche. It was invented by someone at the Guild and can only be viewed using the organisation's own app.'

'Wow, that's cool.'

He points to another person, a woman apparently staring straight ahead of her. The only thing odd about her – apart from this behaviour – is her glasses, which are larger and more clunky than normal. They remind me of the ones an optician uses to test your eyes.

'She's watching an information reel,' Arthur says.

'She's actually watching something?' I say uncertainly. I'm not sure if he's teasing me.

'Yep. Those glasses she's wearing are another Guild invention – the Spectacular. The lenses are really tiny screens.'

'Wow,' I say again. Then I lean forward. 'So, what's the case?' I ask again eagerly.

'Oh, you'll like this one,' he says. 'It's about the National Gallery.'

'Seriously?'

'I'm always serious about art,' he says. I look at this boy – with his floppy blond hair and dimples – and can't imagine he's ever serious about anything.

He draws a sheet of paper from the folder the professor gave us.

'This is Dr Elizabeth MacDonald, the director of the National Gallery,' he says, showing me a newspaper clipping of a woman standing in front of *Sunflowers*. She's an elderly lady, in a tweed skirt-suit with loafers and is dwarfed by the large canvas. Her white hair is pinned back in a neat bun. She resembles a kindly nanny from a children's book far more than the director of one of the most famous art galleries in the world.

'OK . . .' I say, scanning her clothing, her stance and her expression. I don't believe you can work out much about a person from a photograph – especially a posed one, when they're on their guard – but a person's choice of dress says a little about how they *want* to be seen. And how a person desires to be viewed offers certain hints regarding the way they feel about themselves. Elizabeth MacDonald, I decide, is clearly secure enough in her knowledge and experience of the art world not to feel the need to resort to designer clothing or outrageous dress, in order to make her mark.

He draws another sheet from the file: a square photograph.

'And this is Sheila Smith, the senior curator.' The picture shows a woman with wavy blonde hair and bright-red lipstick. He places a one-page document below the image. 'And *this* is the report on her disappearance.'

I look up sharply. This is the first time he's lost his jovial tone and seems genuinely grave. 'Disappearance?'

'That's right. She was reported missing yesterday morning, by Dr MacDonald – although it seems that no one's seen her since Friday night, when she failed to board a flight.'

I take a moment to process this. 'How long have you been working on this case then?'

'I'd only just started when I met you at the Van Gogh yesterday. I'd come straight from a meeting with Dr MacDonald. In fact, I had thought I'd be teamed up with Sofia. Between ourselves, I was quite relieved when she had to fill in for someone who's off sick. She's a bit . . . uptight, if you know what I mean?'

I laugh. 'So, where was Sheila meant to be going?'

He draws out a notebook from his rear trouser pocket and consults his notes. 'Colombia,' he replies, 'to view a painting that's just come on the market. The National Gallery's interested in buying it. It was the art dealer over there, in Bogotá, who called Dr MacDonald on Monday morning, to say Sheila had never arrived.'

'Has anyone checked if she boarded the plane?'

He nods. 'Dr MacDonald made enquiries with the airport. It was a late-night flight – eleven o'clock – but Sheila never checked in.'

'What about her family?'

'They haven't heard from her.'

'Why didn't someone just call the police?' I ask. 'It sounds like a straightforward missing person's case.'

'Ah. The police aren't convinced there's "foul play" involved. They say Ms Smith is perfectly within her rights to take off without notifying anyone. They did have a quick check of her flat, and there was no sign of a struggle. Also, her passport's missing, so she could have gone anywhere – by ferry, if not by plane. They said they're happy to hand it over to a private investigator for now, which is why Dr MacDonald contacted us. There's an agreement that we must tell the police if we turn up anything serious. And they said they'll have to intervene if we haven't found her by Friday evening.'

'We need to get a move on then,' I say. 'What else is in that folder?'

'Not much – it's waiting to be filled. Oh – I'm meant to give you this.' He hands me a fake ID badge, with my name beneath my photo and a company name.

'Who are Prodigal Investigations?' I ask.

'That's our undercover employer, while we're working this case. It avoids awkward questions about the Guild. The story goes that we've been recruited by a PI agency that specialises in hiring promising young people. It's just to show to anyone who asks too many questions.'

'Fair enough,' I say and stash the badge in the outside pocket of my backpack.

He skims through his notes. 'What I found out from my tête-à-tête with Dr MacDonald was that she's approaching retirement, and that she's from an old Scottish clan who own lots of land. They even have an island! It's called the Isle of Fairhaven. She's planning on going to live there when she retires from the gallery.' He puts on a pretty convincing old lady's voice – complete with Scottish accent – and says, 'I'm going to pass the autumn of my years on the Isle of Fairhaven.'

I laugh. 'Is that what she sounds like?'

'It is, and that's what she said, verbatim, when I interviewed her yesterday.' He slips back into Scots mode. 'She's such a dear, wee little thing.' If I'm honest, part of me is a bit uncomfortable about his mockery of Dr MacDonald (I've been on the receiving end of too much teasing myself) but I can't help laughing again – he's too funny.

'Her own island,' I murmur. I picture the tiny plot of land in the Serpentine, to which I've rowed from time to time, and wonder how big the MacDonald clan's isle might be.

'So where do you think we should start?' he asks me.

I'm flattered that Arthur thinks enough of me to ask my opinion, when he's clearly the more experienced agent. I do a mental run-through of important early procedures, from a book I've read five times: *Complete Crime Scene Investigation Handbook.* It tells you that one of the first things is to think of the obvious, and so I say, 'Have you been to Sheila's home yet, to search for clues?'

He shakes his head. 'No. I haven't really started yet.'

I draw Sheila's photo close for a good look. She's probably in her early fifties, dressed in a trouser suit, with one hand in her trouser pocket. With her glossy, blonde, shoulder-length hair, she has a vintage-film-star quality, like Greta Garbo or Rita Hayworth.

'When was Sheila last seen?' I ask him. 'I mean, I know it was Friday night, but what time and where?'

'At work. She got her coat at five thirty and said goodbye to all the staff. Apparently, she prides herself on knowing the names of all her colleagues, on both the art history and art maintenance sides.'

I like the sound of Sheila.

'And did anyone witness her leaving through the main entrance?'

He consults his notebook. 'No. The person on reception was busy with a tour group, so nobody actually saw her go.'

'So she might have been kidnapped directly from the gallery.'

'Or she might even still be there,' he suggests.

'Either hiding, for some reason, or tied up by an assailant.'

This sounds unlikely to me. 'Surely someone would have come across her by now, if she was being kept hostage in the building.'

'A good investigator doesn't rule anything out,' he says.

'True. So we need to check the security cameras to make sure she did leave, and see what time it was.'

'Good idea.'

I Change Channel and summon up a view of the National Gallery, with its roof removed, as if I'm floating above it. If I was Sheila Smith and I wanted to hide here, where would I go? And if I was her assailant, where would I put her, alive or dead?

It takes me a moment to realise Arthur is speaking to me. 'Hello? Earth calling Agatha . . .'

'Sorry!'

'Where did you go?' he asks.

I blush. 'I just switched off this room inside my head and shone a light inside the gallery building.'

Most of the time, people look at me politely or

with mild concern when I explain my Change-Channel mechanism. Not Arthur, though. 'Oh – I do that!' he says enthusiastically. 'I call it Auto-Focusing!'

'Changing Channel!' I say. I catch his eye and we laugh.

'I guess the Guild attracts a certain brand of weirdo,' he says.

'I prefer "maverick",' I say. 'You know – someone who's happy to do things their own way.'

He grins. 'OK. Maverick it is. Let the investigation begin!'

4.

ALL THE SIGNS POINT TO NOWHERE

Arthur and I agree to start our search at the gallery. He calls ahead, to get clearance from Dr MacDonald for us to view the CCTV footage and speak to some of the attendants who were around on Friday.

'So, does everyone who works there know she's gone missing?' I call to him as we cycle through the tunnel network towards Trafalgar Square. The wind's strong in this section, causing my bike to make a strange whistling sound, as if it's alive.

'They should do. Dr MacDonald made a staff announcement. Tread a bit gently, though, in case anyone missed it.'

Above ground, I return my hired bike to one of the public racks close to Trafalgar Square, while Arthur chains his to a lamppost. Then we walk across Trafalgar Square, past Nelson's Column and the four giant black lions on their pedestals, and stride up the steps to the gallery and through the revolving doors.

At the reception desk, a man in a National Gallery T-shirt is fielding enquiries and directing visitors to the various rooms and exhibits.

'Hi,' says Arthur, when it's our turn. 'We should be on your list to visit your security office.'

The receptionist only appears a little surprised to be confronted by a pair of school-age investigators. Dr MacDonald must have forewarned him. He consults a clipboard. 'May I have your names?' he asks politely. We hand over our fake ID badges.

'Ah, yes – I've got you here. The security manager says you're to go straight to the security office. It's here,' he opens a folded gallery map and draws a black ring round a room set in a distant part of the building. She's let the security guard on duty know you're to be helped with whatever you need.' He hands us security passes. 'These will get you through the doors.'

'Thank you,' we say politely.

Before we head off, I ask him, 'Were you here on Friday, at around five thirty?'

He nods. 'Why do you ask?'

I lower my voice. 'You've heard about Sheila Smith?'

'Yes – it's very worrying. As I told Dr MacDonald, I was on the desk, but I didn't see Sheila. She normally says goodbye, but on Friday afternoon I was tied up with a party of tourists. They were rather lively,' he says ruefully.

'Don't worry,' says Arthur. 'It sounds like you had your hands full.'

'We're going to do everything we can to find her,' I assure him.

He shoots me a doubtful look. 'I don't mean to be rude, but you do seem quite young . . .'

'Oh,' I say quickly, 'don't worry – we'll report back to our manager.'

We move off, leaving him to deal with the queue that's formed behind us.

We turn left, then right, before heading down a long corridor and through some staff doors that require us to scan our passes, and I realise that Arthur isn't consulting the map – and he isn't following me.

'Do you know the way?' I ask.

He looks slightly embarrassed. 'Er . . . yeah. I have this ability . . .'

'To remember routes you've only seen once?'

He stops short and turns to look at me. 'You too?' he asks.

'Yep.'

'So that means we both have the Auto-Focus/ Change Channel thing and the map-memory trick . . . What else do you reckon we have in common?'

'I don't know,' I say. But I'm looking forward to finding out.

I can't remember ever meeting someone so similar to me before. I've tended to be resented – rather than celebrated – for my unusual brain. Even around Brianna and Liam, I sometimes avoid stating exactly how I know things, and just let them call it a 'hunch'. Photographic memory and mental filing cabinets only make sense to people whose minds work in a similar way – and there aren't many of us around.

The security office has floor-to-ceiling black double doors with a keypad set into one of them. We press the entry buzzer and look up at the closed-circuit cameras trained on our spot.

Then lights flicker across the panel of the keypad, the door opens, and we're confronted by a large man – almost a giant – in a dark-blue uniform. He must be close to seven foot, with spiky black hair that makes him appear even taller.

'And you are . . .?' he demands.

'Agatha Oddlow and Arthur Fitzwilliam,' I say quickly, just in case my colleague tries any pranks that get us barred from entering.

We show our passes, and the security guard holds the door ajar while we enter.

'I'm Darren,' he says, after we're safely inside the room. He stares at us until I grow a little uncomfortable. At last, he says, 'How old are you two?'

'I'm not sure that's relevant,' says Arthur. 'We're both here on Dr MacDonald's authority.' (I have to admit to feeling quite important when he says that. I stand up straighter and hold my head a little higher.) Arthur holds up his security pass, but Darren just shrugs and peels his gaze from us. He walks over to a desk, where he leans down to input information into a computer. He's not exactly friendly.

I glance around the room. There are no windows, and it's fairly dark. One whole wall is dedicated to a set of small screens linked to cameras inside the different rooms.

'Which day's footage did you need to see?' Darren asks.

'The reception area, on Friday, from around five twenty-five pm please,' I say.

'That's late,' he says. 'We close at six and final admission is fifteen minutes before that. There wouldn't have been many people coming in so near to closing time.'

'We'd still like to see it, though,' I say.

Darren shrugs again, and types the requested date and time into the PC.

'Done.' He points to the screen that's bottom-right in the stack, and Arthur and I walk over to it.

'That must be the party of tourists who distracted the receptionist,' says Arthur, indicating a horde of middle-aged people reclaiming their bags and coats from a man and woman, who are presumably their tour guides.

'Who's that?' I ask, pointing at a figure in a man's fedora hat and a long coat, walking past the tourists.

'I can't see their face,' says Arthur. 'Can you?'

We squint at the screen, but the person doesn't turn towards the camera. They stride out of shot, heading for the exit.

'Do you think it might be Sheila?' I ask.

Arthur turns to Darren, who's busy scrutinising the bank of CCTV footage. 'Darren, how do we rewind this? Can we do it on the screen itself?'

The security guard comes over and shows us the correct buttons to rewind and pause, and Arthur takes the video back to the point at which the unidentified character appears. 'Is this Sheila Smith?' he asks Darren.

Darren joins us by the screen again, and studies

the images for a moment. 'It could be,' he says at last, 'but I wouldn't like to say for sure. Why?'

'I'm sure you've heard that she's gone missing,' I say. 'We're trying to track her down.'

'*You* are?' He sounds like he's trying not to laugh.

Arthur rolls his eyes. 'I know we're young, but we're highly experienced investigators.'

'It's definitely a staff member,' I continue, ignoring the Darren's rudeness. 'See there.' I point to a centimetre of ribbon, showing at the back of the person's neck, just above their coat collar. 'Do you see a glimpse of one of the gallery's security lanyards?'

'Good eye!' says Arthur approvingly, and I blush. (Since when did I start blushing all the time? It's mortifying.)

'Well, if they're a member of staff, I'd say it's definitely Sheila,' says Darren. 'Nobody else dresses quite like that! I haven't seen a fedora since those old films with Cary Grant.'

'She does have her own style,' I say, admiring the hat and the long coat. 'I can't wait to meet her.'

'She's certainly an interesting woman,' says Darren.

'I hope she's all right. The gallery won't be the same if anything happens to her. Dr MacDonald may be the director, but Sheila Smith's the one everyone goes to. She's like the warm heart of the place, you know?' He breaks eye contact and starts staring at one of the screens, as if he's embarrassed by his own sentimental outburst.

I catch Arthur's eye and he says, 'Well, we've got everything we need for now – thank you.'

'Please let us know if you think of anything or hear something that might be relevant,' I say. 'And . . . thanks for your help.'

Outside the room, Arthur catches my eye. 'Well, that was intense,' he says.

'It really was.'

'Do you think he's involved?' he asks.

I pause for a moment. 'I don't know. He did seem very protective of Sheila, so probably not.'

'I agree. I think he's genuinely upset that she's gone missing.'

We head back through the staff-only corridors, until we're out again into the public area of the gallery.

'Time to find out if any of the attendants know where Sheila is,' says Arthur. 'Where shall we start?'

'How about the Van Gogh exhibition?'

'Good choice.'

As we walk past the entrance desk, the receptionist calls us over.

'Dr MacDonald has asked if you could go up to see her, when you're finished with your interviews.'

'Will do,' says Arthur. 'Thanks.'

At the entrance to the exhibition, Arthur turns to me. 'How about you take this one, and I interview someone else?'

'Good plan. Meet you by the reception desk in twenty minutes,' I suggest, 'and we'll go up to see Dr MacDonald?'

'Great.' He heads off along an art-lined corridor, and I walk once again into Van Gogh's extraordinary world. The artist had a condition known as 'synaesthesia'. This means his senses overlapped – he saw shapes when he heard sounds, for instance. Those great swirls in the sky in *The Starry Night*? They were the result of his synaesthesia.

There's no time to look at or reflect on the paintings today, though. We have a case to solve, and a missing woman to find.

The attendant is sitting on a wooden chair beside the archway that leads to the next room. He's staring into space and nodding his head. It takes me a moment to realise he's listening to music.

'Hey!' I say to him.

As he fumbles with his phone, turning off his music app, I take the opportunity to study him. My eyes flick over him, searching for clues to his personality and interests.

EARLY TWENTIES

Dark hair in a ponytai

Long nails on his right hand.
Guitar player?

'Hi!' he says with a smile. 'What can I help you with?'

I decide to trust my hunch. 'What do you play?' I ask.

'Excuse me?'

'I noticed your fingernails. You play the guitar?'

He smiles. 'Wow, you're observant! Yeah – I'm a third-year guitar student at ACM – the Academy of Contemporary Music in Clapham.'

I study him. 'Rock?' I ask.

'We have to cover everything, but, yeah, I'm more into the rock side than classical or folk. Do you play?'

I shake my head. 'No. I love listening, though.'

He gestures to the art on the walls. 'What's your favourite?'

'The *Sunflowers*.'

He nods. 'They're cool.' He points to the wall opposite his chair, where two paintings of Van Gogh himself hang side by side. 'I like the self-portraits. They're kind of creepy, but fascinating, you know?'

'He was so talented . . .' I pause for a moment,

then say, 'Have you heard the senior curator's gone missing?'

He frowns. 'How do you know about that?'

'I'm looking into her disappearance.'

'*You* are? How old are you?'

I produce the fake ID badge and he takes it and reads it. '"Prodigal Investigations". Is that like a PI firm or something?'

'That's right. They specialise in recruiting young people,' I explain, '. . . but we still report to grown-ups,' I add quickly. 'So, do you know Sheila Smith?'

He hands back the badge. 'Everyone knows her. She's a really nice woman. Very glamorous – she always looks great . . .' He pauses. 'So, what's happening? Are the police involved?'

'They wanted to leave it a few more days – they say there isn't any reason yet to suspect foul play, but they're happy to let us look into it in the meantime, as the family are concerned.'

He looks worried. 'So, do *you* think she's all right?'

I shrug. 'I hope so. There's certainly nothing to

suggest she was attacked.' I get my pen ready for note-taking.

'So, Robbo,' I say, reading his name badge, 'when was the last time you saw her?'

He thinks for a moment. 'Friday, at the end of the day. She came round to say goodbye and check I hadn't gone mad from boredom, sitting here all afternoon.'

'So she was already in her coat?'

'Yeah.' He laughs. 'She was wearing this long coat, with a man's hat. She carried it off, mind – very Marlene Dietrich.'

So that *was* Sheila in the CCTV footage!

'Did she seem all right?'

He starts to nod, then appears to remember something. 'Well, she was a bit on edge, you know?'

'In what way, "on edge"?'

'It's just that normally she gives you her full attention, but on Friday she kept checking her phone and she seemed distracted. It's probably nothing . . .'

'It was worth mentioning, though – thank you. Was there anything else?'

'No. After a few minutes, she just said, "See you on Monday, Robbo".'

'Well, thanks for your help.' I tear a page out of my notebook and scribble down my mobile number. 'If you think of anything else, please give me a call.'

He takes the slip of paper. 'Will do. I still can't believe it . . . Sheila, missing . . .'

I remember Darren and the receptionist's comments on how young Arthur and I were, and want to reassure him. 'I promise I'm going to report back to my supervisors,' I tell him, 'and they're going to do everything they can to find her.'

It's only been ten minutes, but Arthur's already waiting when I reach the reception desk.

'Let's find a quiet spot to talk before we go and see Dr MacDonald,' he says. 'Maybe we can find a space upstairs in the medieval section, where it isn't too busy.'

We walk up the stairs and enter a room where

there are lots of religious paintings in dark colours with splashes of gold.

'So, what did you find out?' I ask him.

'Not much. You?'

'Robbo last saw her at the end of the day on Friday, when she did her usual round of goodbyes. She seemed distracted – she kept checking her phone. He also confirmed she was dressed in the clothes we saw on the monitor.'

'So that was her then, on her way out?'

'Yes. It's good to have that confirmed,' I say.

He nods and consults his notes. 'Emma saw her in the ladies' toilets at five twenty pm. They smiled and exchanged pleasantries – nothing more. I also had a quick chat with the other two attendants—'

'Wow, you're quick!'

'Well – nothing to report, basically, so there was no reason to keep them talking.'

'So, no leads . . .'

He shakes his head. 'We'd better report to Dr Mac. Let's hope she's not expecting any results yet.'

'I'd also like to inspect Sheila's office, if she has one.'

He nods. 'She does. We can get the key from Dr MacDonald.'

We head back down to the main foyer area and from there pass through another staff-only door and take the stairs two flights to the second floor. Arthur's been here before, so he leads the way. As we walk, I tentatively say, 'Arthur – have you noticed anything not quite right about the *Sunflowers* painting since it moved position?'

He shakes his head and looks puzzled. 'No. What sort of thing?'

'Just the colouring . . . I'm probably imagining it. Forget it.' I decide not to mention the invisible A at this point – it might distract us, and Sheila's safety must be our priority.

The stairs end at a landing that's decorated with sketches. I'm pretty sure they're originals by Henry

Moore, who made sculptures for public spaces all over London, including one in Battersea Park and another carved into the wall of St James's Park Underground station.

Arthur leads me down a plush, carpeted corridor – lined with more exquisite, original artwork (is that an actual sketch by Picasso?) – and knocks on a door at the end. A brass plate that reads

ELIZABETH MACDONALD, DIRECTOR

announces it as the office of the person we're looking for. 'Enter,' instructs a soft Scottish voice.

Dr MacDonald is standing behind a huge mahogany desk, which is spread with prints of famous paintings. She's busy moving the pictures around and murmuring to herself, but she looks up at us as we approach the desk.

'Mr Fitzwilliam, hello,' she says.

'Dr MacDonald,' he says politely, 'this is Agatha Oddlow.'

'Hello, Ms Oddlow,' she says, and shakes my hand, looking me up and down. I know what's coming next. 'You're very young to be involved in an investigation, aren't you?'

I'm grateful when Arthur intervenes. 'Agatha has already proved herself, Dr MacDonald. She was responsible for the capture of the Bank of England robbers.'

Elizabeth MacDonald tilts her head and raises her eyebrows, as though impressed. 'Well, thank you both for coming out.' She gestures to the surface of her desk. 'In Sheila's absence, I'm having to work out the hanging order for the next show. It's a long time since I had to plan an exhibition myself.'

'Is that a Hockney?' I ask, pointing to a print featuring a bright-blue swimming pool.

'That's right. It's for an exhibition featuring the major pop art exponents.' She sighs and takes a seat behind her desk, gesturing for us to sit as well. 'So,' she asks, 'do you have any leads?'

'Not yet,' admits Arthur. 'We checked out the CCTV footage, as you know. But it looks as though

Sheila left as normal, at around five thirty. We've interviewed four of the attendants, but they didn't notice anything unusual about Ms Smith's behaviour.'

'Have you been to her flat?' she asks.

'Not yet,' I say. 'Arthur and I are planning on heading over there when we leave the gallery.' I remove my notebook and pen from my backpack and prepare to take notes. 'Do you know if she was heading straight home that day?' I ask.

The director folds her hands on her desk and nods. 'As far as I know. She does attend a yoga class twice a week – but I'm fairly sure that's on Wednesdays and Sundays.'

'Does she cook for herself?'

'Aye, she's a fine cook. In fact, I seem to remember she was planning a paella that night – she'd bought fresh shellfish at the market. She doesn't trust airline food, so she was determined to eat well before she travelled.' I exchange a glance with Arthur – we'll need to check if these ingredients made it to Sheila's fridge. If not, it will confirm our suspicion that she went missing before she reached her flat.

Dr MacDonald sighs. 'I'm concerned I may already have left it too long.' Her voice breaks and she looks down, trying to hide her distress. 'I keep asking myself, what if something terrible's happened to her?'

'I'm sure she's fine,' says Arthur.

I wish I shared his confidence. We haven't found any trail to follow – so far, at least – so how can he be so certain?

'If she's alive,' I say, 'we'll find her.'

'And if she's not?' asks Dr MacDonald in a tiny voice.

'Then we'll find out what happened to her,' I reply. 'Can we take a look around her office, while we're here?'

'Certainly.' The director rummages in a drawer and brings out a keyring with a leather tag and a single key. I take it from her and promise to return it shortly.

Sheila's office is at the end of the passageway. The key doesn't turn as easily as I'd expected. I draw it out and examine the keyhole. It's a little damaged.

'Look,' I say to Arthur, who steps up to see more closely.

'Someone's forced an entry?'

'I think so. The lock looks pretty beaten up, doesn't it?'

'We don't know, of course, whether that's a recent thing, though.'

'No, but it's worth bearing in mind,' I say. The more I find out, the more uneasy I am about Sheila's welfare.

With a bit of force, I manage to turn the key in the lock and gain entry. However, Sheila's office is just as I'd expected it to be: neat and organised, with nothing obviously out of place. There's a colourful rug on the floor, a white desk in front of the window, and white bookshelves along the right-hand wall. On the left, a long row of dull-grey filing cabinets is enlivened by a set of small prints in clip frames on the wall above.

Arthur strides over to the desk and begins sifting through the drawers. Meanwhile, I stand still and scan the room, searching for anything I can see that's out of the ordinary. Anything, anything . . .

I walk over to the pictures on the wall. There are eight in all. Six are pop art reproductions – comic-style pictures, in bright colours without shading or subtlety. The other two don't seem to fit. One is *Sunflowers*. The other shows a lake reflecting the hills beside it. It's in vibrant colours – blues, greens and pinks. I'm fairly sure it's by Georgia O'Keeffe. Neither of these two fits with the jokey, cartoony style of the pop art from the 1950s and 60s. I wonder if Sheila might have been using this wall to give herself a feel for the next show. If so, it looks like she lost focus partway through.

'What do you make of these?' I ask Arthur. He comes over.

'Slightly unusual group, but I guess an art curator would have eclectic tastes.'

'Hmm, I guess . . .'

He goes back to searching the desk and filing cabinets, and I fish out my mobile phone, turn it on, and take a photo of each individual print and one of the grouping as a whole.

'Got everything?' he asks, as he shuts the final filing cabinet drawer with a neat click.

'Yep, I think so.'

'Not much to go on, is there?' he says. 'Come on, let's get these keys back to Dr MacDonald and head out of here.'

The director is on the phone when we knock on her door, but she calls for us to enter and gestures for us to leave the key on her desk, which we do. As we turn to leave, she covers the receiver and says, 'Do let me know if you find anything, won't you? I'm worried sick about Sheila.'

'Of course we will,' I assure her, but I can't help worrying that any news we turn up might not be good . . .

5.

INTO THIN AIR

'I know we need to discuss our next move, but I have *got* to eat something. How about lunch?' suggests Arthur as we head back downstairs to the entrance hall.

'Sounds good: I'm starving.' I check my watch. 'It's one o'clock – where did the last three hours go?'

Outside, the day is drab and grey, but the cold wind has dropped at least.

Over toasted sandwiches at the Café in the Crypt beneath St Martin-in-the-Fields church, we take out our journals and compare notes. It's a pretty fruitless exercise. but you never know when something will spark an idea.

I bite into my cheese-and-tomato sandwich. It's steaming, and the hot cheese sticks to my tongue and starts to burn. I take a swig of water.

'So we've talked to some of the attendants,' I say, 'and, apart from Robbo saying Sheila was a bit on edge, none of them noticed anything unusual.'

'I was thinking it might be a good idea to visit the shops around her flat next,' says Arthur. 'I'm hoping one of the shopkeepers might have spotted her on Friday evening, or over the weekend, and be able to give us a shorter time slot for her disappearance – or even have witnessed something useful.'

I nod. 'Good idea. We can tie it in with visiting the apartment. Do you have the keys?'

'No, but I was reliably informed that you were an expert lock-picker.'

'"Expert" might be pushing it, but I've got my tools with me,' I say, patting the backpack at my feet. 'We'd better get a move on.'

'Is your dad expecting you back at a set time?'

'Just after school – he doesn't know I'm not actually *in* school.'

'Aren't you worried the school might contact him?'

'I'm relying on the fact he never hears his phone when he's working in the park.'

'How on earth do you manage to conduct investigations without arousing his suspicions?' Arthur asks.

'I don't. There wasn't much to tell him when he went off to work this morning.' It occurs to me that Dad isn't going to like me being involved in another case. I decide not to worry about that for now, because we need to focus on finding Sheila.

'What about your parents?' I ask Arthur.

'They're not around much,' he says.

'Out of the country?'

'Something like that,' he says vaguely. They sound like Liam's and Brianna's parents. I can't imagine what it would be like seeing so little of Dad. Arthur swallows the last of his sandwich and stands up. 'Ready to get going?'

I take a final bite of my toastie, down the last of my water and grab my backpack. 'Ready.'

Sheila's flat is in Westbourne Park. We take the Bakerloo line from Piccadilly Circus to Paddington, where we switch to the Circle line. In less than thirty minutes, we're standing outside her building.

'Let's start with the shops directly opposite,' says Arthur. 'They're the ones with the best view, so the staff there are more likely to have seen her.'

Our first stop is an optician's. They have a screen behind the window display, which would block their view of the street, but we go inside just to check she didn't call in that day. Although she's a customer there, they say, they haven't seen her since her last appointment, three months ago.

'Greengrocer's or butcher's next?' I ask, as we step back outside.

'Shall we take one each?' he suggests.

I opt for the greengrocer's. There's a queue, and when I reach the front the shopkeeper is clearly irritated by my enquiries.

'Excuse me,' I say, 'I was wondering if you saw this woman on Friday?' I show her a picture of Sheila, which I got from Arthur. It's a copy of the one in the case file.

She huffs. 'If you're not going to buy anything . . .'

'I'll have that aubergine,' I say quickly to appease her. Even as I say it, I'm wondering what I'm going to make with a single aubergine. The fridge was looking pretty bare this morning, and I don't have enough cash on me to buy peppers and courgettes for ratatouille.

'So, what do you want to know?' she asks, placing the aubergine into a brown paper bag and taking my coins.

I hold up the photo again. 'Do you know this woman?'

She nods. 'That's Ms Smith,' she says. 'She gets her fruit and veg delivered every Friday. Normally, she's in when we call round, but our delivery guy said she didn't answer her door on Friday evening. He had to bring the box back, and she never came for it.'

'What time does he deliver?'

But the woman has already moved on to the next customer. She pauses for a moment, as if in thought, her hand buried in a crate of mushrooms. 'Around six thirty. She's his last delivery of the day, to give her time to get home. She works at the National Gallery, you know.' She says this with a hint of pride, as if she's taken some part herself in Sheila's successful career.

'Is she well liked?' I ask.

'Ms Smith?' She looks surprised. 'I don't know her well enough to say. Everybody here gets on with her, though. She's always got a friendly greeting and a pleasant smile.' She frowns, as if suddenly registering my nosiness. 'Who are you, anyway?'

'Oh, just a family friend. I'd arranged to visit her today, but there's no reply at her flat.'

'Well, I hope she's all right,' says the shopkeeper.

I can't think of anything else to ask, so I thank her and leave. Arthur is waiting outside, gazing into space.

'I was beginning to think you'd been kidnapped,' he says. Catching sight of the paper bag in my hand, he asks, 'Anything nice?'

'An aubergine.'

He bursts out laughing. 'Well, you're just full of surprises, aren't you, Agatha Oddlow?'

Not knowing how to respond, I change the subject. 'Any joy at the butcher's?'

He shakes his head. 'They didn't even know her.'

'Maybe she's a vegetarian,' I suggest.

'Or doesn't cook her meals from scratch.'

'No. She gets a box of fruit and vegetables delivered each week, so that can't be right.' Then I remember what Elizabeth MacDonald said as well. 'Anyway – I know she's not a veggie. She'd bought shellfish to make paella on Friday night.'

'So she gets a weekly delivery from the local greengrocer's?'

I nod.

'Had she cancelled this week's delivery?'

'Nope. And all the greengrocer knows is that Sheila wasn't in when they tried to drop her box off. That was on Friday at around six thirty. So it looks like she didn't make it home.'

'Or else someone came to her flat and she left with them.'

'I guess that's possible . . .' I concede. 'It's a very small window of time, though, seeing as she left work at around five thirty and wasn't in for her delivery at six thirty.'

'Shall we visit the rest of the shops in the row?' he suggests. 'They might know something.'

'Sure. I'll take the off licence, and you can take the grocer's on the corner.'

We meet a couple of minutes later. 'Anything?' he asks.

'She bought a bottle of wine on Friday night,' I say. 'The man in the shop reckons it was around ten past six. She didn't seem particularly frazzled or frightened.'

'The corner shop didn't see her – or they don't remember seeing her, anyway.'

'So it's down to whether she made it home with the wine and the paella ingredients.' I rummage in my backpack and draw out my lock-picking kit. 'Come on, let's visit the flat.'

We ring all the doorbells on Sheila's building, until someone buzzes us in through the shared front door.

'Number three's on the ground floor,' says Arthur, pointing down the entry hall.

I stop in front of the pigeonholes for the post and rummage through Sheila's mail. There's what looks like an electricity bill, plus various flyers for local businesses.

'Nothing interesting,' I say.

We walk over to her door, where we pull on latex gloves, so we won't contaminate any evidence. There's only one lock – a Yale-style latch that should be easy to pick. It's one of the first types Mum trained me in. Within seconds, there's a satisfying *click* and we're inside.

'That was impressive,' says Arthur, closing the door behind us.

'Thanks. My mum taught me. It's actually pretty easy.' I pause, thinking about Mum and the uncertainty around how she died. 'She just made it seem like a fun game – we were always playing detectives. Now, though, I keep wondering if she was making sure I had some useful skills, in case her work ever got me into danger and I needed to escape.'

'Wow – that's a lot to think about.'

'Yeah, a bit too much. Anyway, I guess we'd better get on with the case.'

I switch on the light. We're in Sheila's living room. It's a welcoming space, with a blue sofa, matching armchairs and colourful cushions, and a kitchen area along one side. There's a view through French windows of a leafy, green garden. 'Bay trees, laurel and box,' I murmur, approving her choice of evergreens for year-round interest.

'What?'

'Sorry! Old habit, learnt from Dad. Just noticing what shrubs she has in her garden. No use whatsoever to the investigation.'

'Unless she's found a secret passageway to a magical kingdom underneath a bay tree,' he says gravely.

'At this point, I don't think we should rule anything out,' I say, in an equally mock-serious tone.

We both laugh, stopping abruptly when we remember we're dealing with someone's disappearance.

'What if she's in danger?' I ask quietly.

'I'm sure she's fine,' he says. But he doesn't meet my eye. Then he says in frustration, 'There must be a clue somewhere. People don't just vanish into thin air.'

'Agreed. We'll search this flat until we find a lead of some kind.'

'OK – you take the bedroom and I'll start in here,' he says.

'I'd like to see inside the fridge first,' I say.

'Come on, then.' We walk over to her silver larder-style refrigerator, and he opens the door.

'There's a bottle of wine in here,' he says, pointing.

'Yeah, but it's not the one she bought. This is white, and she bought red.'

'No sign of the paella ingredients, either.'

The contents of the fridge are fairly sparse. There's some wilting lettuce in a drawer at the bottom, half a lemon, a block of yellowing Cheddar cheese and a bottle of salad cream.

'So she didn't make it home,' I say.

'No, doesn't look like it,' he agrees. 'Shall we move on?'

I nod and head into the short hallway, where I find two doors. I choose the end one and find I've selected correctly: there's a neatly made bed, plus an antique painted wardrobe in carved wood and a matching chest of drawers and dressing table. This room also looks out on to the garden.

I sit on the bed and gaze around the room for anything that looks *off*.

Poirot joins me. He rubs the top of the chest of drawers with a white-gloved hand and says approvingly, 'She is very clean and tidy, our Ms Sheila Smith.' Poirot is a big believer in order and cleanliness.

'She is,' I agree. *And yet . . . Oh!*

I jump up. Everything in the room is immaculate, with careful paintwork on the walls and doorframe. There's only one thing that doesn't match. The wardrobe door consists of four panels. And the panel at the top right is missing a bit of paint!

I pull up the chair from Sheila's dressing table and

climb on to it. When I push on the panel, hoping it might swing open, nothing happens. But on closer examination, I realise the paint would only chip at the edge like that if someone had used a tool to prise it open. After jumping down, I scour the room for a likely object. And then I see it on the windowsill – a metal ruler, hidden in a vase of dried hydrangeas. Grabbing the tool, I clamber back on to the chair and jemmy the panel open. The whole rectangle of wood clatters to the floor, and I hear Arthur call out to me, checking I'm OK.

'I'm fine!' I call back. I'm staring at the spot where the rectangle of wood fell out. Removing the single panel has exposed a narrow hiding place – a hollow in the door . . .

But it's empty.

I feel a stab of disappointment. I'd been so sure this discovery was going to offer a clue to Sheila's whereabouts! I jump down and grab the wooden panel to put it back. And then I feel something beneath my fingers – an uneven section in the wood. I'm shaking as I turn it over and remove the little plug of wood from the back. There's a folded envelope inside! I sit down on the chair and open it, drawing out a much-folded piece of paper.

'Hey! Come here!' I call to Arthur.

When he runs in, I hold up the sheet of paper. 'Look at this – Sheila had hidden it ridiculously well. I think she must have been really scared for her safety.'

Arthur stares. 'What does it say?'

I read it aloud:

Dear Sheila Smith,

We know you're sticking your nose in where it's not wanted.

stop now or face the consequences! You have been warned ! ! !

'Then there's a signature,' I say, '"The Silver Serpent", and a symbol of a snake drawn in silver ink . . . It's quite pretty, actually – really delicate and detailed.'

'Let's see,' says Arthur.

I hold it up again and he studies it. 'It's not like any snake I've ever seen,' he says disparagingly. 'I mean – the markings are a bit like an adder, but the head's hooded, like a cobra . . .'

I laugh. 'I think that's the idea – it isn't meant to be representational! It can be all snakes, rather than just one specific one. Anyway, what do you think it means? Who could this Silver Serpent be?'

'Someone who didn't much like Sheila "sticking her nose in", apparently.'

'It sounds quite childish to me,' I say.

'Does it?'

'Well, how many adults do you know who tell people not to stick their noses into things?'

'You've not met my mum, have you . . .?'

We both laugh. 'This feels important, though, don't you think?' I say. 'I mean, just the fact that she's gone to so much trouble to conceal it, look—' I show him the wooden panel and the plug of wood.

'Very imaginative,' he says. 'A hiding place within a hiding place.'

'We'd better get on,' I say. 'We can try to work out who this note is from later – and what Sheila was poking her nose into.'

He heads back to the main room and I inspect the note one more time. It's written on high-quality thick paper – and there's a watermark that I don't recognise, but the Guild lab can probably help with that. I sniff the sheet, but any scent it might once have carried has long faded. I put the note carefully into a plastic evidence bag and stow it in my backpack. Then I give the bedroom a detailed search – looking inside drawers and examining the contents of the wardrobe itself. But I just have this gut feeling that I've already found the only thing in the room worth discovering.

Arthur finishes in the big open-plan living room at the same time as I'm done in the bedroom, and we convene in the tiny bathroom.

'I've got something too,' he says.

'What?'

He draws out a clear evidence bag containing a memory stick.

My eyes widen. 'Where did you get that?' I ask.

'It was hidden inside a vase in the living room.'

'What do you think's on it?' I ask.

'I've no idea.'

'Hopefully, it's something less cryptic than the note!'

'Shall we examine it now, on her computer?' he suggests.

'Let's get this room searched first.'

He removes the bath panels while I sift through the bathroom cupboard.

'Anything?' he asks. His head is inside the cavity beneath the bath and his voice is echoey.

'Nope. How about you?'

'Nothing.' He wiggles out and stands up. His hair is full of cobwebs, which he removes with a grimace. 'Fancy checking out the memory stick now?'

'Definitely.'

We walk through to the living room, where Sheila's laptop is lying on her desk. Arthur sits in her chair and presses the button and it starts up quickly.

'Drat! She's set up a password,' he says.

'What shall we do now? Do you think anyone at the Guild could get into it?'

But he's already typing, his fingers tapping too quickly to follow. Codes fill the screen. I watch in awe as the screen, after first turning black, changes to colour – and her desktop appears.

'That was a-*maz*-ing!' I say. 'I didn't know you could hack!'

He grins and bows. 'Just a little extra service I provide, ma'am.'

'Well, I'm very impressed.'

I turn my attention to Sheila's laptop. Her background image is an artwork I don't recognise. It's a large grid of text, all made up of typewriter lettering. At first glance, it looks like the entire piece is formed of the same character, typed over and over again. But when I look more closely, I see there are lots of different hieroglyphic forms as well.

As Arthur goes to put in the memory stick, I say, 'Wait a moment – what do you make of that? Is it just a piece of contemporary artwork?'

'It looks like a piece by Anni Albers,' he says. 'She liked to turn everyday things – like repeated typewritten characters – into works of art.'

I lean over his shoulder and take a picture of the typed grid with my phone. While he loads the memory stick, I home in on the symbols on my mobile. 'There are lots of different characters here,' I say. 'And some of them have been crossed out for some reason. Others have a red background.'

'Maybe Sheila made her own version of an Albers's piece for fun. Anyway, we can look at that later. The memory stick is in. Shall we see what's on it?'

We both watch the screen expectantly. When the laptop has whirred for a while but nothing has happened, Arthur opens the 'This PC' folder and double-clicks on the 'removable flash drive' icon. Again, nothing.

'How is that possible . . .?' I ask Arthur, feeling disappointment creeping in. 'I really thought we were finally on to something.'

'Me too.' He leans back in his chair and stretches out his long legs. 'Why would she bother to hide a memory stick that had nothing on it?'

'I have no idea . . . Try double-clicking the icon again,' I suggest.

Just after starting to move the cursor, he stops. 'Look!'

A word is appearing on the screen . . . It starts off faintly, like a watermark, then slowly solidifies into clear capital letters. We both stare at it.

STOP

'Stop? Stop what?' I murmur. But another word is forming, and now another – and soon a whole message has appeared in the same way, shifting from an unreadable haze into a legible image, like adjusting the focus on a camera.

STOP INVESTIGATING.

AO and AF: WE KNOW WHO YOU ARE.

YOU ARE POWERLESS AGAINST US.

IF YOU WANT TO KEEP YOUR FAMILIES SAFE,

HEED THIS WARNING.

'"AO and AF"?' I say. 'How do they know our initials?'

'I've no idea,' says Arthur.

'So just because they know who we are, they think we'll be intimidated enough to stop our investigation?' I look at Arthur and see he's turned pale. 'Are you scared?' I ask him, keeping my tone neutral so that he won't feel judged.

'It's hard not to be. I've never been threatened before.'

'Haven't you?' I say breezily. 'I'm always being warned off. It's usually a sign I'm getting close.'

He smiles, but it's weak compared with his usual warm grin. 'A bit too close for comfort, perhaps?'

I shake my head. 'You can't let them get to you. They're bullies – and you have to ignore them and carry on, or they've won.'

'Great advice, in theory – not so easy to follow in practice.'

I gesture to the laptop, to point out that they're only words – and then I stop, because the warning has vanished.

'Where did it go?' I say, startled.

He frowns at the screen. 'A self-deleting message!'

'Why would they do that?'

'Well, I guess they figured we can't go running to the police with a blank memory stick . . .'

'Unless the message starts up each time someone puts it in?' I eject it and reinsert it and we wait, but nothing happens. 'I can't believe I didn't take a photo,' I say, feeling embarrassed.

'Never mind. There goes that bit of evidence,' says Arthur.

'We'll get it checked at the Guild lab anyway,' I say, 'just in case there's something about the origin of the memory stick or any fingerprints . . .' I sigh with frustration. 'There must be something more proactive we can do!'

'Stop the investigation?' suggests Arthur.

'You're not serious?'

He pulls a face. 'Of course not – I'm just a bit shaken.'

I put my hand on his sleeve. 'It'll be fine.'

He moves to shut down the computer, and I say, 'Let's look through Sheila's emails while we're here.'

'Good idea,' he says, clicking on her email folder. But Sheila turns out to be as efficient in her tech housekeeping as she is in her office and home – there are only fifty messages. It doesn't take long to sift through them and discover they're all to do with work meetings and gallery arrangements. Her contacts list is longer, though, and we both note down the names.

'There may be something useful in these contacts,' Arthur says. 'I reckon when we get home, we should each see what we can turn up on them.'

'Yes, let's do that. We could cross-reference them with any contacts on her mobile. Do you have a list?'

He shakes his head. 'No one's found her phone. She must have it with her.'

'Has anyone rung it?'

'I did, lots of times. It always went straight to voicemail. And the Guild tried to trace it but failed. Their tech can normally track any phone, even when it's off, but it looks like hers was an ancient model.'

'Not much to go on there then. Let's just see what she's been working on.' I click on the 'Documents' folder and reveal a set of files, all clearly relating to art exhibitions – 'Van Gogh', 'Impressionists', 'Pop Art', 'Cubists', 'Bloomsbury Set' . . .

'Nothing unusual there,' I say. 'We might as well head over to HQ and report to the professor.'

He sighs and shuts down the computer. 'Sure. Do you need to let your dad know you're going to be late?'

'I can text him on the way.'

As we walk back to the Tube station, Arthur asks me, 'What are you saying in your text to your dad?'

'Just that I'm running late.'

'And when you get home?'

I sigh. 'I'll cross that bridge when I come to it.'

Arthur looks at me. 'What if he forbids you from continuing with the investigation?'

'Then I guess I'll be back to sneaking out of my bedroom window and down the oak tree.'

He raises an eyebrow. 'Nobody warned me I'd been partnered with such a rule-breaker.'

I laugh. 'I promise I only break the rules in pursuit of justice.'

I'm pleased to see he's smiling as we pass through the barriers at Westbourne Park station.

6.

DEAD ENDS

Guild HQ is strangely deserted when we arrive back at half past four. I spot Sofia, dashing along a corridor, and run after her.

'Hey, Sofia! Where is everyone?' I ask her.

She pushes a loose strand of hair off her forehead. I've never seen her with anything other than immaculately scraped-back hair before. She even looks hot and bothered, instead of her usual cool, aloof self.

'Hi, Agatha. We're short-staffed since Wallace Jones was apprehended. Various other agents and admin staff have been suspended, pending investigations.'

Wallace Jones had been working for the Guild for years, but he'd revealed himself as a traitor when he and a team broke into the Bank of England. I'd been responsible for uncovering the plot and having him arrested. But I had no idea my investigation would cause the Guild to be short-staffed like this.

'So . . . what are you up to?' I ask.

'I'm on a case,' she says simply. She can be frustratingly brief in her responses. 'But I hear you've been partnered with Arthur Fitzwilliam. Is he behaving himself?'

'Most of the time,' I say. To my amazement, she smiles.

'He's a bit of a livewire, that one,' she says. 'I had to work with him once, and I swore I'd never do it again.'

'Oh, he's not so bad,' I say, feeling the need to defend my new friend.

'If you say so. Speak of the devil . . .' I glance behind me and see Arthur's caught me up.

'Hi, Fia,' he says.

'Hi, Thur,' she says.

'*Thur?*' I ask.

Sofia grimaces. 'If he's going to insist on shortening my name, I'll do the same to his.'

'Fair enough,' I say.

'So, how are you getting on with the case of the disappearing curator?' she asks.

I shrug. 'It's more like the case of the disa*ppointing* curator at the moment – we don't seem to be making much headway.'

'It's only Day One for you, right?' she says.

'Right. But we only have two days left after today – the gallery director wants results by the end of Friday or the police are taking over.'

'Well, if anyone can solve it, Agatha, you can.'

I feel myself blush at this unexpected praise from my former critic.

We stand for a moment in awkward silence, until I say, 'Right, we're off to see Professor D'Oliveira.'

'Oh, maybe I should warn you!' she suddenly says, pulling a face. 'Did you know she'd asked some of the admin staff to help out with Jones's old job until someone new can be appointed?'

I shake my head. Jones had been in charge of ordering in all the supplies that are needed for the underground headquarters, from technical supplies and first-aid kits to coffee and biscuits.

Sofia goes on: 'Well, this poor guy from admin didn't realise that the jars of coffee are supplied in boxes of twenty. So he ordered "twenty", thinking that was how many jars he'd get . . .'

'And he got four hundred,' completes Arthur.

'Exactly! He's made the same mistake with everything – pens, notepads, ink cartridges . . . So the professor *is* around, but she's in a pretty bad mood, trying to find someone more competent to sort out the mess. If I were you, I'd come back to see her tomorrow instead.'

'Thanks for the tip,' I say, feeling deflated.

'See you later,' she says. She gives us a wave and strides off, leaving me staring at her back.

'Wow. I never heard Sofia praise anyone before,' says Arthur. 'You must have made a really good impression.'

'I thought she hated me,' I say in confusion.

'How could anybody hate you?' he says, eyebrows raised.

I hide my embarrassment by becoming business-like. 'Shall we deliver the memory stick and note to the lab?'

He shakes his head. 'The professor might want to see them. Let's see what she says tomorrow.'

'OK. Well, come on – let's get out of here. We can do our separate research into those names, as we agreed, at home.'

'Aye, aye, cap'n!' He salutes me smartly.

'Sofia's right – you're a liability,' I say.

'Ouch!'

'But an entertaining one, at least.'

He grins. 'I can live with that.'

'I was really hoping to talk to the professor, though,' I say. 'I thought she might have an idea about who this threat could have come from.'

We walk in silence. I'm pretty sure Arthur feels the same as me: how frustrating and disappointing today's investigations have been. It feels like we've hit a wall.

As we walk back to the main entrance, I start thinking about the threat again. It is a little scary, but I've been through this before, and I want to reassure my investigating partner, who's looking nervous again. 'Don't worry, Arthur – I'm sure we'll be fine.'

'I hope you're right.' He laughs, but it's a nervous sound. 'I'm not used to feeling vulnerable. I am a trained field agent, of course, but they usually let me focus on the research side of things, where I'm strongest.'

'Do you have any self-defence training?'

Arthur shakes his head. 'The professor did send me to classes, but I don't have any talent for it – I kept tripping over my own feet.'

I feel a pang of concern for him. 'Do you want me to accompany you home, to make sure you're OK?'

He puts an arm round my shoulders in a quick hug. 'That's such a kind offer, but no – I'm sure I'll be fine, thanks. I'm going to stay underground until I'm practically at my front door.'

'Sounds like a plan.'

We've reached the main entrance. I open the door and we both pass through. I point towards the right.

'Well, I'm taking that route, so I'll see you tomorrow. If we each search for those names online, we can compare notes. Shall we meet back here at nine thirty?'

'Can we make it ten thirty? I've got a few things I want to check out first.'

'Sure. See you then.' We part company, each heading in opposite directions.

It's nearly five, so as soon as I can get a signal I send Dad a text to tell him I'm on my way home. Then I begin to jog, replaying the day's events in my mind.

I remember the look on my partner's face as we said goodbye. Poor Arthur. He looked so scared. I wonder if there was anything I could have given him for protection. I run through the contents of my backpack. The trouble is, anything that might double as a weapon for self-defence could also be used against him.

I focus instead on the two items we found in

Sheila's flat. The note is still in my backpack, I realise. I'll have to hand it in tomorrow morning, once I've shown it to the professor.

The lamps are all on when I reach Hyde Park. I keep up a steady pace along the avenues, the skirt of my coat swishing against my legs, until Groundskeeper's Cottage comes into view. Dad's turned on all the downstairs lights, and there's woodsmoke coming from the chimney. It resembles something out of a storybook.

Once inside, I remove my coat, hat and shoes and track down Dad in the living room. Oliver is curled up on his lap and is ecstatic – I can hear his purrs from the doorway.

'Hi, Dad,' I say, but he doesn't look up.

'I got a call from the school,' he says, staring at the blank TV.

I pull a face and perch on the arm of the chair nearest to him. 'Sorry . . .'

'When were you going to tell me you'd started skipping school again? We had an agreement, Agatha. By the time I picked up the voicemail, the school office was closed for the day, so I couldn't even find out how you'd got out, or if they knew where you might have gone.'

'I'm sorry, Dad,' I reply. 'I was going to tell you—'

He interrupts me with a shake of his head. 'How am I meant to keep you safe when I don't even know where you are?' He sighs. 'And how many times are we going to have to have this same conversation? When will it sink in?' He runs a hand through his hair, making it stand on end.

'Is this another one of your investigations?' he demands.

'Um, yes. It's a new case.'

'I don't like it, Aggie. You've got into serious trouble the last times.'

'I'll be careful,' I promise.

'That's what you always say.'

'Don't forget I'm fitter now.'

'Aggie, it's great that you're jogging regularly, but that won't be much good if you get into danger.' Dad thinks I'm just going for regular runs. I haven't told him about my martial arts training, as it would be hard to explain how I came across Mr Zhang and why I don't have to pay for my kung fu lessons. 'You need to attend school,' he continues, 'and not be wandering around the city alone.'

As I open my mouth to protest, he holds up a hand and says, 'I don't want to hear any more about it.'

I give up. There's no point in arguing with Dad when he's like this.

He doesn't stay cross, at least – he pats me on the head as he gets up to cook our dinner. We chat about safer subjects while we eat our fish fingers with Spaghetti Hoops, and then I go up to my room. I get out my notebook, where I wrote down all the names from Sheila's email contacts list, and search for each one online. They all come up easily. Most are people from the art world – curators and restorers, gallery owners, and artists themselves. The remainder seem to be friends from school and university, or family members. If Sheila has a shady alternative life, it's not visible in her online dealings.

Of course it's impossible to tell much about someone from their online presence. After all, my Instagram account is in the name 'Felicity Lemon', who was Poirot's secretary. But on first impressions, it seems unlikely that any of these people would be responsible for our warning message.

I need to sort through the jumble of thoughts in my head. Poirot appears and whispers in my ear, 'One must always proceed with method, *mam'selle.*' He's right, of course.

I turn to the next blank page in my notebook and write:

Where is Sheila Smith?

1. Has she left through choice, or been abducted? Why doesn't anyone seem to know what's happened to her?
2. Who planted the memory stick? How do they know about Arthur and me? Is their threat genuine? If so, what are they afraid we will find out?

3. Sheila had gone to a lot of trouble to hide the note that she received from the 'Silver Serpent'. Who is the Silver Serpent, and why were they threatening her?

4. What is the significance of the pictures on her office wall? Or do they just reflect her personal choice?

Didn't Mum have a reference book on art? I'm sure I've seen one in the living room, and it might help me find out more about the pictures in Sheila's office. I run back downstairs and find Dad sitting in front of the TV, watching a gardening show. It's not one I recognise, and I'm momentarily distracted.

'What's this?' I ask.

Dad smiles sheepishly. 'I'm ashamed to admit it's called *Don't Tell the Owner*. I haven't watched it before, but it seems to involve people doing up their friends' gardens in secret, but instead of it being a nice surprise, the owners are generally horrified by the results.'

'So you're –' I hesitate – '*enjoying* this?'

Dad shakes his head. 'No, I hate it, but somehow

I can't seem to stop watching it. It's like those people that stand and gawp after a horrific car crash.'

'Isn't that what they call it – car-crash TV?'

Dad laughs. 'That makes sense. Anyway, what brings you down from your fortress of solitude?'

'A book. Is there an art book down here, or have I imagined it? One of those reference books about art history.'

'There definitely is one. It belonged to your mum. I think it's on the top shelf.'

I fetch a chair from the kitchen and use it to reach the high-up books. There are various reference works – a German dictionary, a book on the history of music, some volumes of an encyclopedia – and then I see it: *The Story of Art* by E. H. Gombrich. I draw it from the shelf and jump down from the chair.

'You're covered in dust!' says Dad.

'Hazard of the job.'

'Agatha – I hope you're just doing *armchair* investigating!' he calls to my retreating back.

I pretend not to have heard.

7.

A MESSAGE FROM
BEYOND THE GRAVE

When I get back to my room, I find Oliver curled up on my recently vacated desk chair.

I pick him up and reclaim my seat, placing him on my lap. He purrs loudly, kneading me with his claws.

'Hey, boy, stop that – you're hurting me,' I say, but that just makes him purr even louder. I push gently on his bottom, hoping to encourage him to sit down, but he becomes ecstatic, and merely digs his claws in harder. I give up and turn my attention to the book. It's very dusty. I take a tissue and gently wipe the cover of the thick paperback. It doesn't matter how many of Mum's books I've read, there's always something special about holding a volume that was owned by her. A lump forms in my throat as I remember how safe and warm I used to feel sitting in bed while Mum read to me.

Poirot appears beside me. '*Eh bien, mon amie,*' he says, 'now is not the time for sadness. Now is the time to exercise those little grey cells, *n'est-ce pas?*'

He's right. Arthur and I have a mystery to solve, and just two days left to do it – assuming Elizabeth MacDonald doesn't change her mind and alert the police sooner. There's no time to waste on sentimentality.

I start with the index, but I don't know what I'm looking for, so I begin to flick through the book. It falls open quite determinedly in places, as if certain parts of the text have been read and re-read. Focusing on the first spread where this happens, I see that there's a pencil mark beside one of the pictures – a question mark. Turning more pages, I find other pencilled question marks. I search carefully through the volume and count four in all. I take a photo of each of the pictures Mum has marked and then, grabbing my notebook, I log them.

1. *Portrait of Greta Moll by Henri Matisse, 1908*

This painting is on display at the National Gallery. It shows a woman in a high-neck white blouse with her hair pinned up. The sitter was a sculptor and painter in her own right, and a student of Matisse.

2. *The Yellow House by Van Gogh, 1888*

It was only yesterday that I was admiring this painting at the National Gallery!

3. *The Marriage by Hogarth, 1733*

This is from a series of eight paintings, and it's the fifth one, *The Marriage*, that's been singled out.

And then I remember: Mum took me to see these pictures! She explained that a rake is a man of low morals, whose life is filled with drink, gambling and similar bad habits. The paintings represent this man's fall from respectability. The whole sequence is on display at Sir John Soane's Museum – a magical place I haven't visited in years.

4. Man with a Pipe by Paul Cézanne, 1892-6

A quick check on my phone informs me that this is part of the permanent collection at the Courtauld Institute, which is located in Somerset House on the Strand.

I sit back and look at the list I've made.

Why had Mum marked these four? Were they just her favourite pieces of art – pictures she wanted to view, or had viewed? But if so, why did she use question marks to mark them? It hurts to think I'll probably never know.

'Apart from the Hogarth paintings, I don't think these are Mum's preferred artworks,' I tell Oliver, who purrs in approval. 'No – she's highlighted them for some other reason . . .'

I dig out my phone and turn it on, then take a

photo of my notes, which I send to Arthur with the message:

> Hope you're OK. Was wondering what you know about these works . . . Could do with your expertise!

I'm relieved when his response comes almost immediately. I was worried he might have got into a bad state over the threat.

> Means nothing to me. Why? Does this have something to do with Sheila?

> Nope. My mum marked all of these in her art book, but I don't know why.

> Dunno. Could mean anything. Perhaps she just liked them?

> This is Clara Oddlow, Guild agent, we're talking about. She always had a reason.

Good point! 😄
Let me know if there's anything I can do to help

Thanks!

Then I glance through Mum's book for the paintings Sheila had prints of on her office wall. The O'Keeffe isn't there, but *Sunflowers* is, in all its glory. I study it for a moment, but I don't know what I'm looking for. With a sigh, I close the book and am about to place it on my desk when I notice a slight bulge in the back cover. Slowly, I open it again, and examine the thick paper that forms the book's back. There's something there, sealed inside the cover! I fish for a penknife in my backpack, and carefully probe with the smallest blade until the back cover splits open. Inside, there's a folded sheet.

For a moment, I just stare at it. This is something of Mum's – not just a book, but a prized item, something she cared enough about to hide it away.

It sits on my lap – a square of white paper, folded into a neat rectangle.

I take deep breaths to slow my heart. And then I unfold the sheet.

It's a letter, handwritten in indigo ink. The writing is clearly by a keen calligrapher, as it's curly and ornate:

Dear Ms Oddlow,

Further to your enquiries re: The Yellow House and The Marriage, I have made some findings that may be of interest to you. I would like to meet with you to discuss these further.

Please get in touch, at your earliest convenience.

With best wishes,

Samuel J. Cohen, A.C.R.

Freelance art conservator

The Yellow House! Why would Mum have been making enquiries about this Van Gogh painting? And about *The Marriage*, from that series by Hogarth?

And what could be so important or secret that she had to hide the letter away? It's not much, but maybe if I contact this Samuel J. Cohen, I can find out why Mum had written to him and what she wanted to know.

I'm too exhausted to do much else tonight, but I get up and take down the most recent of the red notebooks that contain information on Mum. I use a glue stick to fix the letter to the next blank page. Tomorrow, first thing, I'll contact Mr Cohen. His phone number and email address are at the top of his letter.

Glancing at my mobile, I see I have messages from both Liam and Brianna. It's been less than a day, but I miss having them on hand to discuss the developments (or lack of them) in the investigation.

I send a message on our group chat app:

> Long day. No news on the case. Will write when something happens! Hope all's good with you both xx

Brianna messages straight back:

> **Brianna**
> *Vas-y, mon amie!* Make Poirot proud!

I send a smiley face in response. Then I change for bed, clean my teeth and say goodnight to Mum's photograph. As I snuggle down to sleep, I can't help smiling to myself, and feeling that – at last – I might be a tiny step closer to finding out more about Mum, and what happened to her.

8.

A LARGER PUZZLE

I wake up the next morning, feeling a lot less confident than I had the night before about finding Sheila. It's Thursday already and we only have until tomorrow evening! Last night I completely forgot to look into Sheila's background image for her desktop. With a pang of guilt, I realise that my excitement at finding Mum's letter made me lose focus on the job.

I fish out my mobile, turn it on and study the photo I took of the grid of typewriter characters with, here and there, the hieroglyphic symbols.

There's:

A flower (the background to this is red)
A bird
A mountain
A river
A person
A cat
A house (another red background)
A snail (that one's crossed out).

There are various others, but I stop at the end of the first column. I stare at the tiny symbols, but nothing clicks into place. Sighing, I put my phone to one side, pull on my dressing gown and slippers, and head downstairs.

Over breakfast, I take a deep breath and turn to Dad.

'Dad, *please* can I have the day off school today? It's really important.'

'Agatha, we've gone over this. I won't have you missing school. I'm sorry, but as I said yesterday, you are just a child.'

'But, Dad! I have to do this!'

He holds up a hand to silence me. It's a very un-Dad-like gesture. 'And after "this", there'll no doubt be another "this", then another . . .'

I open my mouth to argue, but suddenly I realise he's right. At least, I hope he is. I can't imagine a life without a stream of cases to investigate.

'I'm sorry,' he says again. 'There will be plenty of time to fling yourself headlong into danger once you've completed your education. Although, obviously, I'd prefer it if you found a less risky profession.'

I nod. 'OK.'

'Good girl.' He stands up. 'Right – I've fed Oliver and he's gone out to torment some birds and rodents.'

'At least he rarely manages to catch any.'

'Fingers crossed.' He kisses my cheek. 'I hope you have a good day in school.'

'Thanks, Dad. I hope yours is good too.' But really I'm on conversational autopilot, planning a way to get out of lessons without alerting him.

As soon as he's left the house, I run upstairs to my room and log into his email account on my computer. I type a message to my form teacher.

Dear Mrs Bodley-Finch,

I regret to inform you that Agatha is very under the weather with a migraine. I'm going to take her to the doctor's later, if there's no improvement. Please excuse her from school for the rest of this week, as she will undoubtedly be feeling weak tomorrow, even if the headache has passed.

Yours sincerely,

Rufus Augustus Oddlow

I feel awful – not about lying to Mrs B-F, as she's horrible, but about deceiving Dad, who deserves better. *I'll make it up to him, when all this is over*, I promise myself.

Then I open my own email app and send Samuel Cohen, the conservator, an email, introducing myself.

Dear Mr Cohen,

You don't know me, but I'm the daughter of Clara Oddlow, who you did some research for seven years ago. You probably know that my mother died around that time.

I've just come across a letter from you, which refers to two paintings, *The Yellow House* and *The Marriage*, saying you had information about both of them. I am anxious to know whether you ever saw my mother, to discuss what you'd found out. Would you be prepared to share your findings with me? I'm trying to piece together some facts about her life, and this would really help.

Thank you!

With best wishes,

Agatha Oddlow

I include my mobile number and press 'send'.

Now back to the matter in hand: there's a missing person to track down.

My phone rings almost immediately with a private number. It seems too quick to be Mr Cohen, but I answer straight away.

'Hello?'

'Ms Oddlow? It's Sam Cohen here. I just got your email.'

'That was quick!'

'Well, I always wondered what happened to Clara. I had no idea she'd died. I'm so sorry. She was a fascinating woman, and very kind.'

'Thank you. It was very sudden.'

Then he says, 'It sounds as though you know what your mother was investigating.'

So it was an investigation!

'Not exactly,' I reply. 'As I said in my email, I just found the letter you sent her . . .'

'Ah, yes.' He's silent for a moment, and I'm about to speak again when he says, 'The truth is, I'm not entirely sure about it myself. That is, I always suspected Clara was investigating a much larger puzzle than she involved me in.'

I sit up. My skin prickles, as if electricity is running along it. 'What sort of "larger puzzle"?' I say.

'That's where I can't help you, I'm afraid. I really have no idea. And she asked me to keep quiet about the work I did for her – otherwise I would have gone to the police. But she said the less I got involved, the safer I'd be. She also suggested I might jeopardise her own investigation.'

Disappointment floods me, filling my eyes with tears. 'So you don't know anything about what she was involved in?'

'I'm sorry, no.' His voice is full of compassion. 'Only the part concerning the two paintings. Shall I email you my findings on those? You might be able to piece together something that I've missed.'

'Yes, please.'

'OK, I'm sending the documents now. I think they're fairly self-explanatory, but give me a call or email me if you want any further information.'

'Thank you so much.'

We say our goodbyes and end the call – and I sit on the edge of my bed, waiting for his email to come through. I can't keep still for wondering whether I'm about to have a huge revelation concerning Mum, so it's a relief when my inbox pings a moment or two later.

There are two attachments and I download them.

Double-clicking on the first, which is titled 'Yellow', I scan the text.

Phrases jump out at me: 'absence of lead', 'yellow too true', and then I read the conclusion:

This is not a Van Gogh painting but a more modern reproduction.

Then I read it again. *This is not a Van Gogh painting*. In a flash, I'm clicking on the other file, where I find a similar report on *The Marriage*. I skip the main body of text and read the last sentence of this one too:

This is not a Hogarth painting but a reproduction, probably painted in the latter part of the twentieth century.

So these two paintings are forgeries! And Mum was investigating them when she died.

I turn to her photo. 'Why were you looking into forged paintings, Mum?' I ask her. 'Is that what got you killed?'

On a whim, I start typing another email to Mr Cohen.

Hello, Sam,

It was good to talk to you. Thanks for these files! I didn't know Mum was researching forged paintings.

I was wondering . . . I know Mum asked you not to tell anyone, but did you contact the police or any art authorities in the end, when you didn't hear from her for so long?

I pause and think for a moment, then add:

Also, do you know if there's anything unusual about the *Sunflowers* painting that's currently in the Van Gogh exhibition at the National Gallery?

I pause again, before adding:

Or an O'Keeffe landscape of a lake with a reflection of hills?

I check my watch. If I'm quick, I should still have time to swing by the National Gallery, to take another look at *The Yellow House* in the light of the new information from Mr Cohen. And if I'm really quick, I'll also make it to Sir John Soane's Museum before I'm due to meet Arthur at HQ at ten thirty.

I layer up for the November weather. Despite the bright sun, I know it's still going to be close to freezing.

Thermal leggings and long-sleeve tops make a great base layer – you can wear anything over them. Flicking through the garments on my racks, I choose one of Mum's old shirt dresses with a gorgeous pattern of sunflowers, which reminds me of the Van Gogh painting. My red coat and matching beret top it off and my Doc Martens boots are well broken-in – they should be good for hours of wear.

Outside, it's bitterly cold – the wind has kicked up another notch – and I catch two buses to the National

Gallery, rather than walk across town. Once through the doors, I head straight to the Van Gogh exhibition. Despite the fact it's a flying visit, I feel much more relaxed now I haven't got the Rathbones, senior and junior, circling like well-trained sheepdogs.

I take a brief detour via *Sunflowers*, and confirm to myself that the flowers do look a slightly different colour from when they were in their old spot, and that the mysterious fancy A is still there in the corner when I shine my ultraviolet torch. Why would anyone mark a painting like this? I surreptitiously flicker the light on the neighbouring pictures, but they are still graffiti-free. I wonder if it could be as simple as that – a graffiti artist, having a laugh?

Then I head over to study *The Yellow House*, passing by Robbo the guitar-player's chair, which is empty this morning. This isn't a painting I'm familiar with, in the way I know *Sunflowers*. The background of the picture shows a steam train passing by on a bridge, set against a very blue sky, with the house itself in the foreground, pale yellow with green door and shutters. I stand in front of it for several minutes, taking in the details – two women with a child crossing the street, people sitting at a table outside a cafe. My expertise doesn't come close to being able to say whether this is a forgery or not. It's a beautiful painting, and it would definitely have fooled me.

Rummaging in my backpack, I draw out the ultraviolet torch and direct it over the canvas. I have to run it across the whole painting twice, backwards and forwards, before I see it.

An ornate capital, just like on *Sunflowers*. So someone appears to be marking the fakes – if that's what they are. Is the A their own initial, or does it refer to something else? I check my watch and realise I need to get a move on if I want to make it to the museum after the gallery.

As I near the attendant's seat, I see it's now occupied, not by Robbo, but by a woman with blonde hair worn loose to her shoulders. She's reading a book. Walking over, I catch her eye.

'Hi,' I say. 'I don't think you were here yesterday, when my colleague and I were interviewing gallery staff, about Ms Smith.'

'Who did you say you are?'

'Oh, I'm sorry!' I produce my fake ID badge. 'I'm Agatha Oddlow. I'm a private investigator, working for a firm that specialises in hiring young people.'

She looks doubtful. 'And they take on trainees as young as you?'

I shrug. 'Only if we can prove we're dedicated and have the right sort of skills.'

She smiles. 'Fair enough. So what's going on with Sheila? Did she really not catch her flight?'

'No, I'm afraid not, and she's not answering her mobile phone or responding to emails either. Sheila Smith's family are worried about her, so Dr MacDonald has hired my firm to look into it.'

'I didn't even know she was going away, until she sent out the email to all staff. It was a last-minute trip. Did you know the painting she was going to view was by the artist she based her doctoral thesis on, Lucy Tejada?'

'No,' I say, shaking my head, 'I didn't know that.'

'Sheila loves Tejada's work – there's no way she'd miss an opportunity of having a private viewing of an original, and possibly securing it for the National Gallery. Is it possible she just caught a different flight?'

'It looks like she didn't check in at all, I'm afraid.' I pause, then ask, 'How did she seem on Friday?'

'A bit distracted maybe, but pretty much like normal. And she does have this big exhibition to organise, right on the back of the Van Gogh. It's not the best time for such a desirable artwork as Tejada's to come on the market, to be honest.'

'Is the "big exhibition" the pop art show?' I ask.

'That's right.'

'I saw she has some prints on her office wall. Do you know if they're anything to do with the pop art exhibition?'

'Yes, they are. Before any big exhibition, she always puts up a few prints or photos of major pieces that are going to appear in the show. It's quite informal –

she says it helps her get a feel for the theme, having some of the more important pieces up round her room while she's planning it.'

'I was a bit confused, though . . .' I say. 'Can I show you?' I dig out my phone and she waits patiently while I turn it on. I call up the photo of Sheila's office wall, and pass it to her.

'Oh! That's odd,' she says. 'Those were all pop art the last time I was in her office.'

'So the Van Gogh and O'Keeffe . . .?'

'I've no idea what they're doing there.'

'Do you know anything about them?'

She shakes her head. 'Sorry. I like art, but I'm no expert. You'd have to ask Sheila . . .' She looks suddenly serious. 'You don't think something bad's happened to her, do you?'

'I honestly don't know . . . There's no evidence of any struggle at her home, which is a good sign.'

She nods, but doesn't look any less worried.

'OK, thanks for your help –' I squint at her name badge – 'Danielle.'

'Danielle Jackson. Let me know if there's anything I can do to help.'

'I will, thank you.' I scribble down my number and pass it to her. 'And please call me if anything occurs to you, however small.'

'I will,' she promises.

It's less than twenty minutes' walk to Sir John Soane's Museum from the gallery. I decide to brave the cold. There's something about the rhythm of walking that can help to process thoughts.

It's as I'm passing the Royal Opera House, and see the name arranged in a grid of neat lettering on the banners, and the stone frieze of dancing figures behind the portico, that something occurs to me.

I stop and pull out my mobile and study the artwork grid from Sheila's desktop again.

What if the symbols represent different paintings? The flower symbol, for example, could be *Sunflowers*. I glance down the column. The mountain could be the mountain in the painting by Georgia O'Keeffe, with its hills reflected in the water. What about the snail? Could that represent the famous collage by Matisse? As it's crossed out, perhaps that means Sheila didn't need to worry about it any more – maybe she'd found out the artwork was authentic and not a fake. On the other hand, maybe the red squares behind the flower and the house mean she'd discovered those pieces were forgeries.

I'm becoming more and more convinced that Sheila had stumbled across something – a forgery ring perhaps? – and her disappearance could mean that she told the wrong person.

Sir John Soane's Museum is in Lincoln's Inn Fields, in the area of central London that's known for its law firms, and it's nothing like any other museum I've ever been to. Rather than enormous rooms of glass cases in rows, imagine a big old house, with interesting things to see on every shelf, every wall and every patch of floor space.

Today, though, I'm determined not to be distracted by all the treasures on display. No, my focus must be on the *Rake's Progress* series by Hogarth – and in particular number five in the series, *The Marriage*. It was one of the images highlighted in Mum's art book, and so it's possibly another forgery. The series contains eight paintings about a young man called Tom, who inherits a lot of money, but wastes it all and ends up with nothing; the fifth one shows Tom marrying a rich old woman just for her money.

One of the amazing features of the gallery is how Soane crammed extra artworks into quite a small space. He fitted hinged wooden panels round the walls, which can be opened up to reveal more paintings hung behind them. I remember that *The Marriage* is hidden behind a panel like this.

One of the attendants approaches. She's a tall, slim woman – verging on bony – with shoulder-length dark hair and deep-blue eyes (I estimate they're shade 13 on my eye-colour chart). She has a streak of purple on one side of her hair.

She smiles at me. 'Can I help you?' she asks.

'I hope so! I need to view the *Rake's Progress*

paintings by Hogarth. Please could you open up the panels for me?'

She shakes her head with regret. 'I'm sorry, but we only open them every two hours. If you can wait another hour and twenty minutes . . .'

I make a show of checking my watch. 'I really can't!' I say. 'I've got a school project on Hogarth due in tomorrow, and I need to check something about *A Rake's Progress* before I hand it in. Please, can you help me?'

She grimaces. 'I really can't—'

'There's hardly anyone else here,' I point out quickly. 'And I promise I won't tell, if you don't.' She still doesn't look convinced, so I add, 'My teacher says I'm going to fail this year's coursework if I don't do a good job with this project.'

At this, she glances around nervously, then nods.

'OK then. But you really mustn't tell anyone, or I'll get into big trouble.'

'I won't! Thank you so much!'

She fetches a short hooked pole and walks over to the gallery wall, where framed portraits and landscapes fill every space. It's like a magic trick when she opens the secret compartment and reveals a hoard of other pictures. All the paintings from *A Rake's Progress* are fixed to the back of the panels.

'You mustn't touch them,' she warns.

'Of course not,' I reply.

These works date back to 1733, and I hold my breath as I lean in to look more closely, not wanting to contaminate the surface. *The Marriage* is . . . different from the others. I try to work out why that is, and in the end I realise it's because it's slightly brighter.

'Was this one moved at any point?' I ask.

'I think it had to be cleaned, around seven or eight years ago,' she says. 'You're noticing that the paint is lighter, are you?'

I nod. 'Why weren't the others cleaned at the same time?'

'Oh – it was something to do with one of our patrons, Lord Rathbone.'

I freeze at the name. 'He suggested just this one painting be cleaned?'

'As far as I remember, it was because this one had become mildewed, whereas the others weren't affected.'

'And did Lord Rathbone pay for the cleaning?' It sounded really strange.

She nods. 'Mmm, that's right.'

'Did he fund any other restoration work?'

'On other pieces in the museum, you mean?' She considers for a moment. 'I think there was a sculpture – but we don't seem to have that on display any more. And there was a Turner landscape as well, where some of the paint was damaged and needed careful reconstruction.' She looks hard at me. 'I thought your project was on Hogarth, though.'

'Oh, it is. But Lord Rathbone's a governor at my school and I know his daughter . . .'

She smiles. 'What a coincidence! Such a charming man.'

I gesture to *The Marriage.* 'May I take a photo?'

She looks so horrified you'd think I'd asked if I could spray-paint graffiti on it. 'Oh, no! We don't allow any photography in the museum. You may make a sketch, if you like.'

I resist pointing out that this wouldn't let me see the contrast between *The Marriage* and the other seven paintings in the group. So I say, 'You've been really helpful,' – and I mean it.

It's hailing when I step out of the museum. The sky is dark grey, plunging London into a curious, premature twilight. I pull up my coat collar and set off, almost jogging to the Tube station. My beret protects the top of my head, but ice trickles down the back of my neck.

As I rush along, I Change Channel, blocking out my discomfort and homing in on the all-important questions about Mum:

1. Had Mum been investigating a ring of art criminals?
2. Did she die because whoever was behind the art fraud wanted to stop her?

I couldn't help wondering as well what Lord Rathbone had to do with it all.

It's a relief to reach the station. A train comes almost immediately and I spend the short journey running through the list of art pieces highlighted by Mum in her art book. There were only four works, but seven years or more have passed since she put those question marks in her book . . . If my hunch is correct, and each one of those paintings is a fake, who knows how many other priceless artworks could have been stolen and replaced with fakes since then?

Then I think about Lord Rathbone – smug, complacent, self-important Lord Rathbone – and about what the attendant has just told me about *The Marriage*. It's puzzling why he wanted that particular painting cleaned – one of the pictures on Mum's list, and that Sam Cohen has confirmed is a forgery.

Is it just a coincidence?

9

AN ABSENCE OF LEAD PAINT

Arthur's already waiting in the main office corridor when I arrive at HQ. He looks like he's just dragged himself out of bed. His hair's sticking up at the back, and his shirt's untucked in a couple of places.

'Hey! Sunflowers,' he says, seeing my dress, 'like your favourite painting!' I grin, pleased he's remembered.

'Hey, yourself! You look shattered.'

'I stayed up too late, reviewing the file,' he says.

'Did anything occur to you?'

He shakes his head.

'I found out something interesting,' I tell him.

He raises an eyebrow. 'Oh? What's that?'

'The Hogarth painting highlighted in Mum's art book – *The Marriage*, on display at Sir John Soane's Museum – well, I've just been there . . .'

'Yes?'

'Well, it turns out it was taken away for cleaning seven or eight years ago, probably around the time Mum was investigating. And it looks like my mum was on to something.'

'What's that?'

'Forged artwork,' I say.

His eyes widen. 'Really?'

'Yep. Those question marks I found in her old art book were all next to works she suspected of being forged.'

'How did you find that out?'

'I unearthed a letter she'd received from an art conservator, whose conclusion was that *The Yellow House* and *The Marriage* are fakes.'

'What's his name, this conservator? He could be a useful contact.'

'Samuel Cohen. I've asked him if he knows

anything about those two mismatched pictures on Sheila's wall too.'

'Really? Why?'

'Just a hunch,' I say.

'Fair enough.' He taps something into his phone. 'Just making a note, for reference.'

'There's something else,' I say, 'about those two pictures in Sheila's office . . .'

He nods. 'What?' he asks.

'Well, one of the gallery assistants confirmed that Sheila uses that wall to help her when she's planning exhibitions. She's been planning for an upcoming pop art show and had put up prints of pop art pictures. But two of the pop art images had been swapped out, for ones I suspect are forgeries. So I think Sheila had found out they were fakes as well.' I take out my mobile and show him the photo of the grid from her laptop. 'This kind of confirms it, don't you think?'

He raises an eyebrow. 'Am I being slow here? How does a square filled with typewriter characters confirm Sheila was suspicious about forged paintings?'

'Sorry – I forgot to explain! The important things

are the hieroglyphic symbols in the grid – I think these are clues to different paintings. So the flower represents the *Sunflowers* painting, for instance.'

'And the crossed-out snail means "no molluscs allowed",' he suggests.

'I can see you're going to take some convincing, but bear with me,' I say. 'What if that symbol stands for the Matisse collage, and the fact it's crossed out means the collage work is genuine?'

'I guess it's possible,' he says at last. Then he hesitates, as if he's deciding whether to say something. 'Look – there's something that's been bothering me.'

'What?'

'*Sunflowers*. You know how you said it looked different, and now Sheila might also have thought there was something wrong with it?'

'And it has an invisible A.'

He frowns. 'An invisible A?' he repeats.

I nod. 'Yep. That and *The Yellow House* both have a really elaborate capital A written or painted on in invisible ink.'

'How on earth did you find that out?'

'It was Brianna, messing around with my ultraviolet torch.'

'Wow . . . Well, anyway, one of the attendants I spoke to – Liane – said Lord Rathbone had requested a private viewing of *Sunflowers* before the show opened. I wonder why?'

It's my turn to stare. 'Really? Arthur, I didn't tell you – it was Rathbone who arranged for *The Marriage* at Sir John Soane's Museum to be cleaned.'

'Oh? That's quite a coincidence,' he says. 'So he had easy access to *Sunflowers* and showed a special interest in *The Marriage*. There's something else too . . . I found this. It was wedged behind the *Sunflowers* painting, the day I met you.' He passes me something small, pushing it into my palm. I unfurl my fingers and examine the object. It's an engraved cufflink, gold with a white griffon. 'It's the Rathbone family crest,' he says.

I peer at the mythical beast. 'There's something wrapped round it – like a scarf,' I say. I rummage in my backpack for my magnifying glass. Under the powerful lens, the 'scarf' resolves itself . . . 'It's a snake,' I say, feeling my heart speed up with excitement. 'A serpent!'

'Really?' Arthur grabs the cufflink back and I hand him the magnifier. He peers through it for a moment and then looks at me in astonishment. 'You're right!'

'Arthur,' I say, almost in a whisper, 'maybe Lord Rathbone is the Silver Serpent!'

I reflect on where Arthur found the cufflink. Had it merely been lying on the floor, it wouldn't have meant a thing. But *behind* the painting . . . There's no way it could have got there, unless Lord Rathbone had been hanging the picture himself or, which is more likely, given his inflated sense of self-worth, telling others how to hang it. I can just imagine him getting in everyone's way, while believing he was crucial to the whole operation.

'Why didn't you show me this earlier?' I ask him.

'I didn't think it was relevant. I was just planning on handing it in to the receptionist – but I kept forgetting. And now you're telling me *The Yellow House* is a forgery, and you're wondering if *Sunflowers* might be another one, as there's a print of it hanging on Sheila's office wall . . .'

'I can't believe it,' I say, '. . . Lord Rathbone.'

'I thought you couldn't stand the man.'

'I can't, but I still can't really believe he'd be involved in forgery and art theft.' I sigh. 'Well, let's report to the professor and see what she has to say about all this.'

As we start walking, someone comes round the corner – a familiar figure, with her dark hair scraped back in a ponytail.

'Sofia!' I call.

'Agatha, hi!' She walks over and looks as though she's about to say something, but seems to change her mind.

'Still stuck here?' I say.

'Yep. Right here, just like yesterday. I'm on desk duty again – research and admin.' She lowers her voice. '*Very* dull.'

'What happened to your case?' I ask.

'Oh, we're so short-staffed, we're all having to take turns with the tedious stuff. My partner's off doing the legwork, and we'll swap over this afternoon. I can't wait – I'm not made for sitting behind a desk.'

'And is the professor in her office?' I ask.

'She should be. She was in a foul mood yesterday, though – you did well to avoid her.'

We say goodbye to Sofia outside Professor D'Oliveira's office. Our boss answers promptly when we knock, and we go inside.

'So, you're here at last,' she says, looking from Arthur to me. 'You do realise Dr MacDonald is expecting an outcome by tomorrow?' She glances at the clock on her wall. 'You're aware it's already mid-morning on the penultimate day of the investigation?'

'We would have reported to you yesterday, but you were busy,' I say.

She frowns. 'What time did you come by?'

I hesitate, unwilling to bring up something we knew she felt was a waste of her time. 'Oh, just in the afternoon . . . But we heard you were caught up with a problem to do with office supplies.'

'Oh—' She stops abruptly and frowns. 'You heard

about that silly mix-up? Yes, that did take me a while to sort out.'

She gestures for us to sit down, so we take seats side by side facing her.

'So where are you up to with the National Gallery disappearance?' she asks.

'We've talked to the attendants and receptionist, and viewed the CCTV footage,' I say. It looks like Sheila Smith did leave as usual, at five thirty on Friday.'

'She made it back to Westbourne Park, where she lives,' continues Arthur. 'We've had confirmation of that from a local shopkeeper.'

'Right,' says the professor. 'So did she enter her flat?'

'That's where the trail goes cold,' I say. 'She wasn't in at six thirty for a delivery, and there was no sign of any disturbance in her home. The groceries she'd bought aren't in her fridge either.'

'But we did find this,' says Arthur, placing the bagged memory stick on Professor D'Oliveira's desk.

'A memory stick? Where did you get this?' She

begins pulling on latex gloves to remove the item from its bag.

'Hidden in a vase in her living room,' says Arthur.

'At first, we thought it was from her,' I add, 'some kind of message. But we plugged it into her laptop, and it had a warning . . .'

While I've been speaking, Professor D'Oliveira has inserted the memory stick into her own computer. We wait expectantly.

'There's nothing on it,' she says at last, looking at us for an explanation.

'There was,' says Arthur.

'But it vanished,' I explain. I close my eyes briefly and Change Channel, so I can summon up the image in my mental filing cabinet. Then I open my eyes and say, 'It read: "Stop investigating. AO and AF: We know who you are. You are powerless against us. If you want to keep your families safe, heed this warning."'

The professor scribbles the message down on a notepad and studies the words.

After a moment, she looks up. 'Any idea who this could be from?' she asks.

'Maybe,' I say, and I draw out the note I found in Sheila's flat. 'There's also this.'

She picks it up, still in its evidence bag, and scrutinises it.

'Any scent?' she asks.

I shake my head. 'The paper's good-quality though – it has a watermark,' I point out.

She holds the bag up to the light and nods. 'Quite a standard one, unfortunately – I don't think the lab will be able to make much of that. But you say you have a theory, Agatha?'

'Yes – we think Lord Rathbone is the Silver Serpent.'

'Lord Rathbone, the art patron?' She sounds very surprised.

'That's right.'

She frowns. 'What makes you think he's involved?'

'Arthur found a cufflink behind the *Sunflowers* painting, and it has the Rathbone family crest on it.'

Professor D'Oliveira looks at Arthur, who fishes the cufflink out of his pocket and hands it over. The professor picks up a magnifying glass and peers at the cufflink. 'Is that a griffon . . . and a snake?'

'A silver serpent,' says Arthur.

'It's a bit tenuous, don't you think?' she says, putting down the cufflink and magnifier.

'It would be,' I say, 'if there wasn't further proof he's involved.' I fill her in on our suspicions about the forgery ring – first, the reports on *The Yellow House* and *The Marriage* that Sam Cohen had prepared for Mum, and his conclusions; then the mismatched pictures on Sheila's wall; and, lastly, the fact that it was Lord Rathbone who had *The Marriage* removed for cleaning.

The professor goes quiet as she listens.

Eventually, she says, 'The possible links between what Sheila had uncovered and your mother's investigation aren't solid enough to pursue at present. Let's just focus on finding Sheila for now. We'd better see what comes up from inspecting the memory stick and the warning note to Sheila. Is there anything else?'

We shake our heads.

'Drop the memory stick and note off at the lab now. And one last thing,' she says. 'I would advise you both to take the necessary precautions, and not to do anything needlessly risky.'

I'm not very sure what counts as 'needlessly risky', but I decide not to ask, in case it rules out anything I might want to do.

After saying goodbye, we head off towards the laboratory. Arthur knows its location so he leads the way. At the lab, we check in the evidence, although Arthur decides to keep hold of the cufflink. 'We might need it to challenge Rathbone,' he points out.

'Now, do you fancy a hot chocolate before we do anything else?'

'Arthur, we've only got until tomorrow evening to track down Sheila. I don't think going for hot chocolate fits into the schedule.'

'If we have it here, we can discuss our next steps while we drink.'

'Here?'

He stares at me. 'Has no one shown you the canteen?'

'There's a canteen?'

He looks astonished. 'Did you not get your induction tour?'

I shake my head. 'I just got Sofia showing me the induction room. Does that count?'

'No, it does not. Come on – we're going to the HQ dining hall.'

I have to focus hard to memorise the route as I jog to keep up with Arthur's long strides. Left, left, right . . . through an unmarked door . . . down a short flight of steps, and through double doors into . . . a room like nothing I've ever seen – or certainly not below ground.

If I hadn't got used to suspending my disbelief, I'd have trouble believing this place was real.

The canteen is huge. At least a hundred tables of varying sizes and shapes are spread out in a room filled with plants. We're far from daylight, yet thriving greenery hangs from the ceiling and stretches up towards the roof. Guild staff sit around, reading, chatting, eating and drinking.

'Wow!' I say.

'Cool, huh?' He's wearing a smug expression as if he designed and built the dining room himself.

'Very cool,' I say.

Arthur waits until we're seated with our hot drinks in front of us, before saying, 'I was thinking . . . we should test *Sunflowers* – see if your hunch is right, see if it's a fake.'

I laugh. 'How are we going to do that?'

'It's pretty easy,' says Arthur.

I look at him in surprise. 'Is it?'

'I'm one of the Guild's art experts, don't forget.'

'So what does that mean, exactly?'

'It means, among other things, that I'm issued with the tools to test a painting's authenticity. All I have to do is get close enough.'

'Do you have the tools with you?' I ask.

He unzips his messenger bag and draws out a small black case, which he opens to reveal a neat black machine. It reminds me of those little labelling machines that shop assistants use for pricing, except that it has a small built-in screen.

'Always prepared, like a good boy scout,' he says.

'I don't believe you were ever a good boy scout.'

He grins. 'You're probably right.'

'Is that an X-ray fluorescence spectrometer?'

'You know about these gadgets, do you?' He sounds impressed.

I nod. 'It's like a microscope and X-ray machine in one.'

'That's right. And, as you probably know, it can tell us, among other things, what pigments were used to make the painting. Van Gogh was painting in the second half of the nineteenth century, when they used lead paints. So we're looking for lead. In fact, Van Gogh was known to use lead-based paints – it's the reason for one of the theories for why he painted like he did. He could have had lead poisoning, which caused inflammation of his retinas, so he would have seen circles of light, like halos, around things, like in *The Starry Night*.'

I did know this, but I don't get a chance to say so, as Arthur's enthusiasm is carrying him along.

'Also, did you know,' he continues, 'that he added lead sulphate to *Sunflowers*?'

I put down my mug to give him my full attention. 'Why?'

'Well, he wanted to create a very vibrant, sunny-yellow pigment—'

'But the sunflowers in his picture are dark – almost brown! Or they were, until the picture was moved . . .'

'That's right. They've darkened over time. The lead sulphate reacted with the yellow chromate, causing the darkening effect. Painters already knew there was a problem with some of the brighter shades of yellow back then – but they couldn't work out what was causing the colour to corrode.'

'That's fascinating,' I say.

He studies me for a moment. 'Are you being sarcastic?'

I shake my head. 'No. It *is* fascinating. Also, I just love gadgets. My friend Brianna's got some brilliant ones, including an actual seismograph, for checking tectonic activity.'

'Cool!'

'I know. I've never seen an XRF in action, though.'

'Well, now's your chance.' We grin at each other's enthusiasm.

'You'll be able to look at the invisible A as well, won't you?' I say.

He nods. 'Right: are you ready to be lookout?'

'Ready.' I down the rest of my hot drink and we leave behind the lush interior of the canteen and head back out to the Guild's corridors and tunnels.

It's noon when we get to the National Gallery. Among the Van Gogh masterpieces, I check for potential onlookers while Arthur switches on his little gadget and waits for it to warm up. A couple stroll by, arm in arm, and I smile at them, as though we're just hanging out – rather than about to get up-close-and-personal with one of the most celebrated paintings in the world.

'Anyone around?' hisses Arthur, bent over his spectrometer.

'Just a man, over by the self-portraits.'

'Is he watching us?'

As he asks this, the visitor turns and leaves the room. 'No.'

'Here goes then!'

He holds the spectrometer up to the painting, presses more buttons, and we wait for a few seconds. Some lights flash and then several rows of words and numbers appear on the device's screen.

'Got it!' he says. He zips the gadget back into its bag and we head out of the exhibition and find a quiet section of corridor.

'So?' I ask him.

'Definitely a fake.'

'Really?'

'Really. There isn't any lead in that painting.'

'So Rathbone's an art thief . . .'

'And on a grand scale,' he says. 'It's not like he stole a work by some unknown artist – this is a Van Gogh! His *Sunflowers*—'

I stop abruptly. Although I don't like Sarah Rathbone, I suddenly feel a wave of concern for her. Nobody deserves to have a crook for a father – and what happens if he ends up going to prison?

'We're going to have to confront him,' Arthur says.

Normally, I love the chance of challenging a villain. Right now, though, I realise I have cold feet. I Change Channel for a moment, running through the clues that point to Lord Rathbone being guilty.

'But what if we're wrong?' I say after a moment. 'What if he really did just have *The Marriage* cleaned? What if he did just help with hanging *Sunflowers*?'

'Agatha, the evidence is heaped against him.' He ticks off the items on his fingers, one at a time: 'The private viewing, the cufflink, the cleaning, the serpent in the family crest . . . But I can go and see him on my own, if you're scared.'

I shake my head. 'It's not about being scared of him. I guess I just don't want to confront him in case we're wrong. Think what it would do to Sarah.' I don't say what I'm also thinking – that if Lord Rathbone is involved, then that would also implicate him in my mother's death, and I'm not quite ready to face that.

He studies me. 'I honour that sentiment,' he says, and I feel myself blush. 'But he's involved in a criminal activity, Agatha, that may well result in more deaths.'

'More *deaths*?' I look at him in horror. 'Do you believe Sheila's dead?'

He pulls a face. 'I don't know. It's a bit odd, the way she's disappeared so completely that nobody seems to have spotted her since she bought that bottle of wine.'

I shiver at the thought that our search for Sheila might already be too late. If that's the case, we have to catch her killer!

'OK . . .' Arthur says. 'Shall we go over to the Rathbones' place now and get this over with?'

I take a deep breath. 'OK – let's do it.'

10.

RATHBONE MANSION

It takes us half an hour to get to Chelsea on the Tube. The Rathbone residence is about five minutes' walk from Sloane Square station. We pass the Saatchi Gallery, then I have a moment's pang, realising we're near Chelsea Physic Garden in Royal Hospital Road. I remember visits there with Mum. She loved showing me all the medicinal plants, and explaining their uses. I haven't been there since she died.

'Are you OK?' Arthur is watching me, with concern on his face.

'I'm fine. I've just realised we're near a garden I used to visit with Mum, that's all.'

'It's hard losing a parent. My dad left us when I was five.'

'Do you still see him?'

'No. We never heard from him again. He just took off while I was at school.'

'That's awful!'

'Yeah. For years I hoped he'd just be there again when I got home, with some fantastic excuse for not coming back sooner.'

'At least I knew Mum was dead – I wasn't expecting her to come back. I guess that's been a bit easier than what you've gone through.'

'Both ways sound pretty tough.'

'Do you still hope to hear from your dad?'

He shakes his head. 'I don't want to any more. He had his chance to be a dad, and he threw it away. Mum did a great job of bringing me up single-handed.'

We arrive at a set of enormous metal gates. Arthur presses the buzzer and explains that we've come to see Lord Rathbone, and, no, we don't have an appointment.

I quickly add, 'I'm at school with Sarah.' This seems to be our entry ticket. The gates buzz and swing open, allowing us entry. The house isn't immediately visible – only when we round a bend in the driveway do we catch our first glimpse. The Rathbone homestead is even bigger – and grander – than I imagined. It's ancient, with leaded windows, and there's ivy climbing up its cream façade. There are too many chimneys to count, and massive grounds, with exotic trees even I – who's grown up in a celebrated London park – would have trouble identifying.

'Wow!' Arthur and I say in unison.

'I bet there are wings,' I say.

Arthur laughs. 'What? You think they can fly? I know they're mega rich, but . . .'

'No – I mean the house. I bet the house has wings. You know – North Wing or East Wing, that kind of thing.'

'I'm sure you're right. Hardly seems necessary for one family to own such a mansion, does it? Imagine how many people you could house in this place.'

A butler meets us in the hall. He doesn't smile,

but he also doesn't turn his nose up at these uninvited guests.

'Sir, madam – if you would follow me, please. Lord Rathbone has asked me to show you to the Red Wing study.' Arthur and I exchange a knowing look.

We walk for what seems like five minutes, but is probably no more than a minute and a half. Then the butler shows us into a room and leaves us. For a moment, I think he's going to lock us in, but he only shuts the door.

'Did you tell the Guild?' I whisper to Arthur.

'What? That we were coming here?'

I nod.

'Nope. Did you?'

I shake my head. 'My phone's turned off at the moment. Can you page them or something?' I ask. 'It might be quicker.'

He pulls out a gadget that looks like a small phone and keys in a message. 'Done,' he says.

I feel better immediately, knowing the Guild will be able to track us down if necessary.

The door opens and Sarah Rathbone walks in.

'Hello, Oddball, what are you doing here? Sammy on the gate described the strange girl who was trying to get in, and I felt sure it must be you.'

'You were right,' I say simply.

'So what are you doing here?' she says again. But before I need to answer, the door opens again and Lord Rathbone strides in.

'Thank you, Sarah, that will do,' he says.

'But I want to know why *she's* here,' insists Sarah.

'I will find out and tell you later – *if* that is appropriate. Mr Fitzwilliam and Ms Oddly—'

'Oddlow,' I correct him, but the cold look he shoots me makes me wish I hadn't. If looks could freeze . . .

'Mr Fitzwilliam and Ms Odd*low* have come to speak with me in private,' he tells her.

Sarah tuts loudly but leaves the room, although I wouldn't be surprised if she's still outside, with a glass to the wall.

'Please,' says our host, gesturing to two high-back armchairs. We sit down and he takes a seat behind his desk, which is mahogany and even bigger than the professor's. I glance around the room, taking it all in.

The study is large – about twice the size of my attic bedroom at home. There's a large grey stone fireplace and the wallpaper has a bold pattern of gold and red stripes. The artwork is also large and imposing. One shows naked people being tortured in hell – *lovely* – and another depicts a man herding elephants. *Colonial* is the word that comes to mind. This is clearly an old family that believes it deserves its wealth.

But not when you come by it illegally, I add in my mind. Poirot appears at my shoulder, studying Lord Rathbone closely.

'I do not like this gentleman, *mon amie*,' he says after a moment. 'He is not, I fear, a decent human being.'

I feel the same way. I remember that awful, predatory grin I witnessed at the gallery on Tuesday, and barely suppress a shiver.

'So to what do I owe this honour?' Lord Rathbone consults his watch, presumably to make clear how precious his time is.

'Something came up,' says Arthur, 'and we wanted

to give you the chance to respond before we go to the police.'

I'm disconcerted to see that our host looks amused, rather than rattled.

I decide to try another tack to throw him off balance. 'We found something that belongs to you.' I hold out the cufflink.

'You've got my cufflink!' he exclaims. 'Where on earth did you find it?'

Arthur doesn't chip in, so I volunteer the information. 'It was wedged between one of the paintings at the National Gallery and the wall.' I watch him closely.

Rathbone's eyes narrow. 'Which painting?'

'*Sunflowers*,' Arthur says.

I add, 'The forged *Sunflowers*.'

At this, our host unexpectedly sits back in his chair and roars with laughter. I catch Arthur's eye and we exchange a look of confusion.

'Why is that funny?' I ask.

'Forged? *Sunflowers*? Ha! One of the most famous paintings in the National Gallery's permanent collection? Don't you think someone would have noticed? The curators, for example?'

I wait for him to stop laughing. Then I say, 'I believe Sheila Smith *did* notice.'

Arthur clears his throat. 'We've been wondering what you had to do with the forgery and with Ms Smith's disappearance.'

'I beg your pardon, young man? Whose disappearance?' Lord Rathbone looks bewildered.

'Sheila Smith's,' I retort, 'senior art curator at the National Gallery. As a patron of the gallery, I'm sure you know her.'

'She's been missing since last Friday evening,' Arthur continues. 'Is this really the first you've heard of it?'

At this point, Lord Rathbone turns the same shade of red as I'd observed on our school trip. From this vantage point, I can confirm that it is indeed colour #9A0000 in the hexadecimal code – although right now I have rather more urgent concerns, such as the alarm button he's just pressed.

'You have a nerve,' he says angrily. 'You come

into my house and accuse me of forging masterpieces and abducting some woman I've only met once or twice at gallery functions? How dare you, the pair of you!'

'But your cufflink . . .' I say. I look at Arthur, who nods in encouragement.

'I lost that cufflink two weeks ago, when I attended an event for patrons at the gallery. I have no idea how it got stuck behind a painting, but I can only imagine someone thought it was a good joke.'

'What about my mother?' I ask. I doubt I'm going to find out anything now, but I have to ask.

'Your mother?' he says, and now he looks genuinely confused. 'What on earth has she got to do with it?'

Just then, the door opens again, and a man in a security guard's uniform appears. 'Sir?' he says.

'Yes, Giorgio. Please escort these two visitors off the premises.' He looks from me to Arthur and back again. 'You are not welcome to return, unless *invited* – do you understand?'

'Well, that didn't really get us very far,' says Arthur, as we watch the gates buzz shut behind us. 'I really thought he'd crack.' He gestures for us to walk, and we start back towards the Tube.

'Do you think it's possible that Lord Rathbone isn't involved after all?' I suggest. 'He was angry – but not alarmed or frightened. He didn't behave as if he's a master criminal who's just been found out.'

'He probably thinks we're just kids, and so we don't pose a threat.'

'I don't know,' I say. 'I mean, he must be aware that I was involved in getting to the bottom of the bank heist . . . It was in the papers, and his daughter is at school with me.'

'Well, it doesn't look like we'll get another audience with him for a while. But we should tell the Guild about our meeting. They might want to do some behind-the-scenes investigating of Lord Rathbone themselves.'

Without warning, he stops walking and stands very still, gazing into space. I reckon he's Auto-Focusing, so I give him a moment. After a while, he blinks and then he's back with me. It reminds me of someone coming out of a hypnotic trance. I wonder if I look the same when I'm Changing Channel.

'Well, whether or not Rathbone's involved, you're right about one thing,' he says. 'It's too much of a coincidence that Sheila's replaced two of her pop art pictures with at least one forged one.' He pulls out his mobile and types something in. 'Shall we check out the Georgia O'Keeffe landscape, to see if that's been forged too?'

'Won't it be in the States? I think most of her work's over there.'

He shakes his head. 'The Tate Modern's hosting a major exhibition of her work.'

I stare at him as the pieces of the puzzle start to click into place. 'How long's it been on?'

'At least a month.'

'So Sheila could have visited . . .?'

'Absolutely.'

Excitement is fizzing inside me.

'What's the quickest route to the Tate Modern from here?'

11.

A KNOTTY PROBLEM

Arthur points to an old brick wall, covered in ivy.

'There's a gate through there,' he says.

'Just like in *The Secret Garden*!' I say. 'I've always wanted to find a door like that one.'

He grins. 'I know – it's great, isn't it?'

We wait for a couple of joggers to pass, then duck under the green foliage. The vine screens us completely, reminding me of the secret area behind some waterfalls. There's not much room in this magical space, however, and Arthur hastily pulls out his Guild key and unlocks the gate. We pass through and into complete darkness.

'Mobiles out!' he says. I rummage for mine and

turn it on. The two narrow beams do little to brighten the blackness. I shiver. We're in a corridor that slopes down. It's hard not to run, pulled along by gravity, but I lean my weight back, determined not to trip over in the gloom.

'This tunnel's definitely one of the creepier ones,' says Arthur. His voice is muffled.

'Will we be out of it soon?'

'Yep. There's a bend any minute, and then we join a main passage that's level.'

Sure enough, the slope evens out almost as soon as he finishes speaking, and we step round a corner and into a wider tunnel. Here, our mobile phones give far better illumination, reflecting back from pale, whitewashed walls.

I check my watch. It's just after two. 'Do we have much further to go?' I ask, suddenly conscious that we've only got a day and a half left.

He catches my eye. 'Do you fancy a run?' There's a definite challenge in his tone.

'Always,' I say.

He takes two head torches from his bag and hands

one to me. I fit it and switch it on; the beam is white and very bright.

'Ready?' he asks me, as we line up, and I nod.

'And . . . go!' We take off. I pace myself to start with, getting into a comfortable rhythm. Arthur shoots ahead, but I wonder how long he can keep up that pace. He's out of sight, but I can hear his feet pounding against the hard earth.

'I'm coming for you!' I shout.

I round the next bend but there's no sign of him. I stop, listening hard. There's loud breathing a little way ahead. 'I can hear you!' I call. He doesn't answer, and I start to feel unnerved. It's so dark, outside the beam of my torch, and I shiver, feeling suddenly isolated and vulnerable. 'Stop it, Arthur – it's not funny!'

Then I hear a scream – Arthur's voice. I start to run towards him, but there's someone else here and I'm jerked backwards as my arms are caught and twisted behind my back.

I shout out, but a cloth bag is pulled over my head, muffling my voice.

'Arthur!' I shout. But I'm shoved through a door

(I hadn't even noticed a door in the dark tunnel), then dragged up a flight of stairs. 'Arthur!'

I hear him scream again. What are they doing to him?

There's not enough air inside the bag. *I can't breathe, I can't breathe . . .*

And then Poirot appears, a friend in the darkness.

'*Eh bien, ma petite*, this is a sticky situation, *n'est-ce pas?*'

I slow my breathing as I'm yanked along. *Focus, Agatha, focus.*

Who's taken me?

It occurs to me that it's only a short while since we accused Lord Rathbone of being a master criminal. Now he's getting his revenge. This must be what happened to Mum. I hate the thought that her final moments may have been so awful. But I can't let my emotions take over right now.

I will escape, I promise myself. I'll get away – and free Arthur too – and then we'll rescue Sheila together. Rathbone will be arrested, and sent to jail, and we'll make sure he knows it was us who reported him. Maybe I can finally get justice for Mum.

I hear a vehicle door being opened, then a rough hand pushes my head down and I'm forced inside. I land on a seat, but I'm lying down and can't get upright with my hands tied behind my back. The rope's tight and my arms feel as if they're being pulled from their sockets. I try to breathe into the pain, rather than fight it. This helps a bit, but not enough. The engine starts up. I can hear two voices – a man and a woman talking in low, urgent tones.

'Arthur?' I whisper, checking he's here.

'Agatha – are you all right?'

I'm torn between relief that he's alive and (selfishly) that I'm not alone – and regret that he's been captured too.

'Yes. Are you?'

'They banged my head when they put me in the car and it's throbbing. I'm OK apart from that, though. Where do you think they're taking us?'

'I don't know. Maybe if we're quiet we can follow the route.'

'OK . . .'

We stay silent. At first, I keep track and have some idea of our whereabouts. But the journey is longer than I expect, and the road becomes bumpy – we've turned off the official roads and on to an unmade road – possibly a country track.

I whisper to Arthur, 'Have we left London, do you think?'

'I don't know. My internal compass doesn't seem to work in the dark.'

'Mine's malfunctioning big-time.'

'Maybe we can get some idea when they take off our hoods,' he says.

'Maybe . . . Do you think we could fight our way out of this?'

'I know I couldn't.'

'Hey! You back there! Stop talking!' It's the female captor.

We fall silent again. The car starts to slow down, then it comes to halt. A moment later, the door is opened and I'm yanked back out. My arms are throbbing with pain and I'm worried I might pass out. *Focus, Agatha*, I tell myself again.

I stumble as I'm pushed along a path. The man and woman are murmuring to each other as they march us. I catch the woman's name, 'Sals', and something about a 'waste of time . . .'.

Then I feel the surface change from packed earth to concrete beneath my feet. We're inside a building. My hood's removed and I stand, blinking in fluorescent light. Behind me our captors leave, and a key turns in a chained padlock.

It's impossible to make anything out at first, but as my eyes focus, I see my partner lying on the ground close by.

'Arthur! Are you OK?'

He groans and I stagger over to his side. Crouching down, I inspect him. He looks pale.

'I'm all right,' he says.

'You don't look it.'

'It's only my head – it's still hurting.'

'Let me get you untied . . .' I take a recce of our surroundings:

HiGH CEiLiNG WiTH
WOODEN BEAMS

Concrete floor

Brick walls

Boarded-up windows

BLADES OF STRAW AND
DIRT/DUST UNDERFOOT

SOME RUSTiNG FARM EQUiPMENT
iN THE FAR-RiGHT CORNER

Only one point of entry/exit –
and that's just been locked
by our kidnappers.

It's obviously an old barn or outbuilding.

'No,' says Arthur.

'No, what?'

'No, I don't want you to untie me.'

I stare at him. 'Why not?'

'Because we need to look passive – let them think

they're in control. If we break out, they're much more likely to hurt us.'

I consider this. 'You're probably right, but I don't plan on still being here to get caught after we're free.'

'Agatha – you don't even know where we are. We could be in the middle of nowhere.'

'Can you drive?'

He shrugs. 'I've done some off-roading.'

'So, if we can get their car started, we can escape.'

'Right – so now we're hot-wiring a car . . .'

'How hard can it be? I've studied basic mechanics . . .' I look at him. 'What's your idea then?'

'I was thinking we'd act as if we're going along with everything. Then, when their guard's down, we'll attack.'

'Attack with what? Last time I checked, you didn't have any fighting skills.'

'No, but I'm a whizz at building traps.'

'Seriously?'

He nods. 'You wouldn't believe what I can do with some broken-down machinery and a bit of imagination.'

'It sounds like a children's programme: "Come on, kids – let's build a human trap!"'

He laughs. 'I'd definitely like to present that show.' He falls quiet. Then he says, 'We're going to be all right, aren't we?' It's not really a question.

'Hey, with your brain and my brawn? We'll be just fine. How about I untie our ropes, just to make us more comfortable? Then we can always make it look like we're still tied up afterwards. It's got to be better to have our hands free, after all.'

He sighs. 'All right. But I'm hiding behind you if it gets physical.' He squints at my joined wrists. 'Are you sure you can undo these? They look pretty complicated.'

'Ahh – but I'm a master knot-unpicker.' I examine the knot in his rope, which I identify as a constrictor. I can picture how to tie it, but it's designed to be a difficult one to unfasten.

'Do you have a knife on you?' I ask him.

'Nope. They took that and my phone before they shoved me in the car.'

'My penknife's in my backpack – and I lost that when they attacked us in the tunnel.'

'You could gnaw through the rope with your teeth?'

It turns out to be very difficult to untie a constrictor knot while your own wrists are fastened behind your back. For a few minutes, I'm like a dog chasing its own tail – there's a lot of movement on my part but no real progress. Eventually, I find a position that allows me to work on Arthur's ropes. It's still a slow process, involving me passing rope-ends backwards, around and forwards.

'Give up yet?' asks Arthur.

'Never.'

A moment longer and the knot slackens. 'You did it!' he says, shaking the cords from his wrists.

'Now can you do me?'

Arthur's vast knowledge turns out not to extend to knots. I have to use the rope he's shed to direct him on how to tie – and, crucially, untie – a constrictor.

A key turns in the lock again, and we both freeze. My own cords are still half-tied, but Arthur's are lying on the ground next to me.

'Arms behind your back!' I say quickly. It seems even more painful to have to hold my arms in place, now they've been loosened. I glance at Arthur and see he's thrown himself back down on the floor, in the semi-foetal position they left him in, with his hands behind him. His rope is out in the open, and it's glaringly obvious.

Our kidnappers reappear. They're both wearing masks, which are a bit unnerving as they hide not just their real faces but also their expressions. The woman stands guard by the door while the man comes towards us. As he approaches, I quickly shuffle on my bottom towards the heap of cord. I use tiny movements and hold my breath, hoping they won't notice. By the time the man reaches me, I'm perched uncomfortably on top of the rope. He looks me over, then examines Arthur before walking back to join his colleague.

'Do you know why you're here?' the woman asks us. Her voice is muffled by the mask.

'You're working for Rathbone?' I say.

'Is that what you've heard?' she says.

'It's pretty obvious, isn't it?' I say.

'So we need you out of the way for a while,' she says. 'Then we'll decide what to do with you.' She and the man leave, turning the key to lock us in again. Despite the cold in here, I'm sweating. I glance down and see that one end of the rope was sticking out from under me.

'That was too close,' I tell Arthur.

'I was sure they were going to spot that the rope was undone!'

'Can you finish untying me?'

'I can try.'

I don't know how much time passes with Arthur attempting to undo the constrictor knot while it seems to only get tighter round my wrists.

'Give up,' I say at last. 'I think you're making it worse.'

'Sorry,' he says. 'Knots really aren't my thing.'

'It's fine.' While I start to work on the knot myself, Arthur stretches and eases his muscles. With one last wriggle on my part, the cord comes loose. I groan in relief as I can finally stretch out my arms and shoulders again. I stuff the rope into my pocket.

'You really are a master knot-unpicker,' he says with a grin.

'Yep. Just one of my many talents.' I smile back, to show I'm not really that conceited.

Arthur says quietly, 'What do you think they're planning on doing with us?'

I don't answer straight away. He needs reassuring, and I don't want to relive memories of my previous experiences. Despite my new martial arts skills, I'm still uncomfortable remembering the tycoon Maxwell's desire to kill me and my friends for the sake of his business enterprises – or Wallace Jones's attempt to drown me in the underground harbour.

At last, I say, 'I don't know, but I think they'd have killed us by now if that was the plan.'

'What do you think we should do?'

'First, we're going to look for signs that Sheila was held here.'

'Sheila?'

'I'm sure these are the same people who took her –

and it makes sense that this is their usual holding area, before they move hostages on.'

'Hostages . . .' repeats Arthur, and shudders.

'Actually, I'm feeling pretty lucky right now,' I say, pushing myself on to my feet despite my complaining upper body.

He stares at me. 'What about *this* makes you feel lucky?'

I shrug and I'm shocked by the painful objection from my arms and shoulders. 'We're actually in the right place. Also, whenever I get abducted, it means things are starting to move in the right direction with the investigation.'

He laughs. 'Only you could talk about being kidnapped like it's a hobby, Agatha!'

I start to comb the floor for signs of a previous prisoner. 'Don't get me wrong,' I say. 'It's never enjoyable. But it's good to know we've rattled someone's cage enough to make them come after us. With any luck, we've unnerved Rathbone enough to make him do something careless.' I search in the general area where we were deposited, then move in small circles, careful not to miss any section. It's dim in the barn, thanks to the boarded-up windows, and I wish I still had Arthur's head torch.

As it turns out, I don't need a light, though. A white rectangle is clearly visible on the rough concrete floor just a metre or two away. As I get closer, I see that it's attached to a black lanyard with the words NATIONAL GALLERY clearly printed on it in white. I don't have my latex gloves or an evidence bag, so I crouch down and use the bottom of my dress as a protective layer between my skin and the ID badge.

Arthur moves to my side and says, 'What have you got?'

I hold up the badge, which has Sheila's photo with the title SENIOR CURATOR beneath it.

'Wow,' he says. 'You were right. She was here.'

'She was here,' I say.

At that moment, the key turns again in the lock, and I stuff the lanyard and badge inside my coat pocket and place my poor, aching arms behind me. I glance at Arthur and see he's made it back to his position on the floor. This time, he's taken his rope with him and it's fully hidden beneath his body.

Our assailants come in, closing the door behind them. I can't see any way I could beat the two of them without Arthur's help. This time, it's the female who walks over. She stops where she can see both of us and says,

'This has been a warning. If you continue to investigate, you will be putting yourselves and your families at risk.'

She scrutinises me in silence, which gives me a chance to examine her in detail – something I hadn't attempted while I was trying to conceal Arthur's rope.

AGE: HARD TO GAUGE WITHOUT SEEING HER FACE, BUT SHE HAS QUITE A YOUNG ENERGY WHEN SHE WALKS, PROBABLY 30–35

Height: five foot eight

Skin tone: part of her neck is visible below the mask – tanned

*Hair: cropped
dark-blond*

BUILD: BROAD AND
MUSCULAR (EX-ARMY?)

I glance over at her associate. He's also got military bearing.

'Why did the two of you leave the armed forces?' I ask.

Despite her training, she has a 'tell' – her shoulders twitch slightly. It's only a tiny movement, but it's enough to assure me my instincts are right. She not only was in the forces, but she's unsettled by her prisoner having this (or any) information on her.

She speaks again. 'As I was saying, your families will be in danger, if you continue your investigations.' There's no mistaking the menace in her voice. 'In your case, *Agatha Oddlow*, that would be . . .' she takes a notebook from her breast pocket and reads, 'Rufus Oddlow, head gardener in Hyde Park.'

'OK –' I hang my head as if intimidated, but I can't

resist getting in one last, hopefully unnerving dig, remembering the name I heard earlier – '*Sals.*'

'Agatha . . .' hisses Arthur. He's still lying on the floor.

I'm treading a narrow line. If I go too far, she's liable to get angry with me.

She takes a step towards me, and her colleague says, 'Don't!' in an urgent tone.

'She knows my name,' says the woman. 'She knows too much about us . . .'

'She's bluffing,' says the man.

'He's right – she is bluffing,' says Arthur. I shoot him an angry look.

Sals swivels and, in an astonishingly smooth move, she has Arthur in a headlock. His face looks startled and terrified.

'Is that true?' Sals asks me. 'Are you bluffing?'

'Don't hurt him,' I say.

'Why not?' she asks, tightening her hold. He whimpers.

There's nothing for it – I have to act. But I realise with a shock that I'm scared. I've been so busy thinking about Sheila, I've forgotten to pay attention to my own physical and emotional state. Now I notice that my breaths are shallow, my palms are sweaty and my heart is beating too fast and too loudly.

I Change Channel, focusing on my breathing and balance, and calming the rapid beating of my heart. (I picture it like a metronome that's swinging too quickly and needs slowing.) What would Mr Zhang have me do? It needs to be a form of what he'd term 'non-violent resistance'.

'Why's she got her eyes closed?' asks the man.

'I don't know . . .' says his colleague.

I have it! My eyes flick open and, in a movement at least as smooth as hers, I leap towards Sals, landing on both feet. We're so close that my forehead is almost touching her chin.

Caught off guard, she steps back, loosening her grip on my friend. It's then a simple task for me to unwind her arm from the headlock and pivot away, escorting Arthur until we're out of arm's reach. This part's a bit like a waltz. I've always done appallingly in ballroom dancing at school, but perhaps I'm not as bad as I thought.

'There's no need for that,' I tell her. 'I'll answer your questions. Yes, I was bluffing. The way you two stand, anyone could tell you're ex-military. And I heard your colleague say your name earlier.'

'How did you two get loose? Those were good knots!' says the man.

But Sals and I ignore him. I hold my breath. Will there be another attack, or have I defused the situation?

'I understand the message from today,' I tell her. 'We'll stop investigating.' I hold out the name badge as a peace offering. If I'm going to show them I'm serious, and stand any chance of getting home, we need to sacrifice this piece of evidence.

'Where did you find this?'

'It was here,' I say. 'Proof that Sheila Smith was also held hostage by you. But if you take it, we've got nothing to take to the police.'

'Good girl,' she says. She glances at the man, who nods.

They throw the hoods back over our heads and tie us up again. This time, the knots aren't as ambitious – they'll be far easier to release.

I cry out as I'm dragged to the car. My shoulders and arms are throbbing so hard, it feels like I've gone several rounds in a boxing ring and come off badly. I wish I could see Arthur and check he's OK, but I can't make out anything through the stuffy head covering.

Lying on the back seat of what I've decided is an old four-by-four designed for off-roading, I'm bumped up and down as we head back along the farm track. I can hear Arthur groaning.

'Where hurts?' I ask him.

'Mainly my head. But my arms are pretty bad.'

'Mine too. I wish they hadn't tied us up again.'

'What was going on back there?' he asks. 'You were really pushing her buttons. I thought she was going to lose the plot.'

'Two things: I wanted to unsettle her – to make her think we knew who they were, so she'd be more likely to believe us if we said there was a rescue party coming to get us. And I wanted to see if I could get her riled, so she'd lose concentration and do something careless.'

'She nearly did – she'd have punched you, I reckon, if I hadn't intervened.'

'You shouldn't have done that. I was getting somewhere.'

'You were setting yourself up for a bruising.'

I sigh and we fall silent. The journey back seems even longer than it did going. Every bump aches and I feel bad for Arthur, as he whimpers close by.

'What if they aren't taking us back?' he says at last. 'What if they're going to kill us?'

'If they wanted us dead, they'd have tried it by now. They just want us scared. As far as they're concerned, we're a pair of kids who'll be easy to scare off.'

'*And I'd have gotten away with it, if it weren't for those meddling kids,*' says Arthur, in a cartoony American voice. I'm glad he hasn't lost his sense of humour.

After what feels like an hour, though I don't

suppose it's really that long, the car pulls over and I'm lifted out and dumped on the ground. I land on my knees and shout, 'Ow!' as I feel small stones bite into my skin. We're outside, at least. That's got to be better than being locked up in another building.

Arthur cries out – so he's obviously had the same rough treatment. But we're about to be free.

When my head covering is removed, I can see he's close by. We're lying in a lay-by. Sals is holding my backpack in her gloved hands – so it wasn't lost in the tunnel! She makes sure she has my full attention and then she unzips my bag and tips the contents out into a muddy puddle, before dumping the backpack on top. Then she climbs back into the car and we watch as the vehicle pulls out.

'Memorise the registration number,' I say, committing it to my own memory.

'Done,' says Arthur. Then he whimpers again. 'I'm freezing.'

White flecks are falling from a slate-grey sky. I shiver. 'That's because we're outside and it's sleeting,' I say. My shoulder wrenches painfully as I use an elbow to push myself into a sitting position. Right: time to cut us both free. I can't face unfastening any more knots, even if these are simpler.

I glance around the filthy lay-by, which is filled with plastic bags, takeaway boxes, toilet paper, an abandoned trolley and an old mattress. I'm going to have to extract my penknife from the puddle. I stumble over and crouch with my back to the muddy pool. After a lot of fishing, I manage to extract the knife and, with my hands black with dirt, I make it back to Arthur's side. It isn't easy to cut ropes when your fingers are frozen, but I keep sawing away until Arthur's trappings fall away. Then he does mine.

We both groan as we rub our arms and shoulders and stamp our feet to keep warm.

'Freedom!' I say. Exhaustion washes over me as the adrenaline rushes out.

'I just realised – you saved my life!' he says.

I frown. 'What are you talking about?'

'When that woman – Sals – had my head under her arm, I thought she was going to squeeze all the air out of me.'

214

'You're forgetting she only put you in that headlock because I wound her up by seeming like I knew too much.'

He shakes his head. 'Even so . . .'

'Even so, what?'

'You put yourself in danger, to help me. Not many people would have done that.'

'Sure they would. You'd do it for me, wouldn't you?'

'I guess . . . I mean, I hope so . . .'

'So do I!'

We both laugh.

'Anyway, I'm freezing,' he says. 'Can we get away from here, please, and into the warm and dry?'

'Good idea.' I fish in my backpack and turn on my mobile. 'There's no signal here,' I say.

He checks his phone. 'Same here. It must be all the trees.' The road we're on is thickly wooded.

'Let's walk,' he says.

I check my watch. It's four forty and I have no idea where we are. 'Shall we just go in the opposite direction from the car?' I suggest.

He nods and we begin to walk.

'I can't believe it's only a couple of hours since we were racing through the tunnels,' I say.

'I know. It feels like everything's changed, doesn't it?'

The occasional car passes us, but we keep in among the trees, not wanting to be spotted.

At last, we see the lights of a building ahead. 'I think it's a pub,' says Arthur.

As we get closer, we see it's a restaurant, with a sign that says THE FOREST FOX. Inside, the owner lets us use her phone and sit near the door until our taxi arrives. She's very concerned about us and wants to know if we're all right, but we just tell her we got split up from a Duke of Edinburgh hiking trip. She's very kind and insists on giving us hot chocolate to drink while we wait. We have a phone signal at last, so we each text our parents, to let them know we're OK.

At last, the cab arrives and we clamber in, weary, cold and damp.

'Where to?' asks the driver.

'We should get you home,' says Arthur.

'It's fine if you want to be dropped off first,' I say.

But he shakes his head. 'No. You deserve to be safely back with your dad.'

'OK . . .' I look at him, trying to gauge his mood – unsure why I deserve this more than he does.

I consider asking the driver where we are, but I don't want to get into a discussion with him about how we got here. I turn on my phone and open Maps.

'We're in Barnet,' I say. 'So it probably does make sense to go to my house first.'

Arthur nods and addresses the driver: 'Greenwich via Hyde Park, please,' and the man pulls out. Arthur closes the communication window to give us privacy. It occurs to me that, if this were a thriller, we'd shortly find out our driver was really an evil henchman. I examine him. He's definitely over sixty – possibly over seventy – and small and wrinkled like a garden gnome. My experience with both the professor and Mr Zhang has taught me not to underestimate older people, but I'm pretty sure I could win against this man if it came to it. Reassured, I settle back in my seat.

My phone pings with an email notification. It's from Sam Cohen.

'What is it?' says Arthur.

'An email from the art conservator,' I say, clicking on it. 'Listen to this: "Dear Ms Oddlow . . ."'

I was extremely interested in your follow-up query, as I've been conducting my own investigations, ever since your mother stopped being in contact. The *Sunflowers* painting appears, to me, to have lightened considerably since its move to the Van Gogh show.

The Georgia O'Keeffe piece you mention is, I believe, *Lake George Reflection*, which recently sold at auction for almost $13,000,000.

I began making enquiries about this artwork, but was interrupted by an unexpected visit from a stranger. I'd better say no more here, but he has certainly left me feeling uncertain of my way forward.

I look at Arthur. 'What do you make of that?'

My companion's sitting with his head back and his eyes closed. He opens them a fraction. 'Of what?'

'The conservator starts looking into the pictures, and suddenly he's receiving warning visits.'

'He doesn't say this visitor threatened him.'

'No, but "left me feeling uncertain of my way forward" sounds pretty worrying, doesn't it?' I pause. 'I feel bad, because it's me who put him on to this.'

'Actually, it sounds like that was your mum, seven years or so ago.'

'But he didn't receive any threats or warnings or whatever till now, did he?'

'Agatha, you can't be responsible for everybody's safety. He's a grown man – I'm sure he'll work something out.'

'I hope you're right.'

'What I don't understand is, why he didn't go to the police over this – if he'd uncovered forged artworks.'

'Mum asked him not to.'

'Why?'

'Well, she was on a case of her own, wasn't she? Maybe she'd discovered the people involved were dangerous, and she didn't want to expose him. Or she needed more proof about their dealings. What if it wasn't just about forged art? Maybe there were other things going on, and the fakes were just part of the investigation.'

'So you think Rathbone's on to him as well?'

'It sounds like it, doesn't it?'

'Or maybe his visitor hasn't threatened him at all – maybe this person just caused him to doubt his findings.'

I smile at him. 'I like the sound of that.'

'Well, until you speak to him, why don't you assume that's the case?'

'I'll try. Thanks.'

'No worries. Are we square now? You saved my life and I made you feel better.'

I pull a face. 'I'm not sure that's a fair exchange. Blood for blood, don't you think?'

'Hey! Who raised the stakes? No one said anything about blood!'

We're still laughing as the cab pulls up in front of the park gates.

I check my watch. It's nearly six o'clock – what a

day! I run through the events. We now know that Sheila was taken by the same people who kidnapped us – presumably working for Rathbone. We also know the kidnappers have a military background. And we have that vehicle registration number . . .

I rummage for money, but Arthur stops me. 'It's fine – I'll claim it on expenses.'

I hesitate. 'I keep wondering where they took Sheila, after that holding place, I mean. I don't think they dropped her off in a lay-by too, do you? Because if they had, she'd be back home by now.'

He nods. 'They must have taken her somewhere else.'

'Or what if they've hurt her?' I say, voicing the elephant in the room.

Arthur winces, then turns to me. 'I don't think that's their style, for what it's worth. They've warned us off the investigation, when they could have really hurt us – or worse.' He gives a tired smile. 'Look, we've done all we can for today, don't you think?'

'You're right. Let's rest, and put our heads together in the morning. We need to be in a good state for our last day on the case. We've *got* to find Sheila tomorrow! I can't bear to think of Dr MacDonald going to the police because we've failed.'

'You're right,' he says. 'Shall we text first thing, to agree where to meet?'

'Sounds good.'

I drag my weary body out of the taxi, thank the driver and wave to Arthur until he's just a blur through the back window. Then I walk slowly along the paths to my home, where I hope my dad will be waiting with a roaring fire.

But there's no sign of him when I get inside the house. Oliver's also strangely AWOL and, apart from a light in the hall, everywhere's dark. *Where's Dad?*

I can't think straight as I run through the hall, throwing open the doors to the kitchen and living room.

What if the kidnapping was a distraction – what if they were after Dad all along?

'Dad!' I almost scream his name up the stairs.

I'm halfway up when I hear him shout, 'Is that you, love?' from the direction of his bedroom.

He's here. He's fine, I tell myself.

Suddenly, I'm exhausted. I make my way slowly to the top, then knock on his door and go in. He's lying on the bed, with Oliver sitting hunched like a snail on his stomach. From the look on the cat's face, he's having a wonderful time. (This is confirmed by his purring, which is nearly as loud as a motorcycle engine.)

'Are you OK?' I ask Dad.

He sits up. 'I'm fine – just having a rest. I've been doing lots of digging today – we dug out some of that area that floods after rain, to form a better run-off, so with any luck that'll be the last of the flooding. You're back late, though.'

'Yes, sorry – things came up.'

'But you're all right?'

For a moment, I'm tempted to blurt out: *No, I've had a terrifying day, in which I was captured and tied up and blindfolded and locked up and threatened. And then I thought something had happened to you . . .* But I take a deep breath and say, 'I'm here, aren't I?'

'Indeed you are. You fancy a takeaway?'

'Pizza?'

He laughs. 'Sure. You order and I'll pay. Does that sound all right?'

'That sounds perfect.'

I walk over and give him a big hug and a kiss on the cheek.

'What was that for?'

'Nothing. I missed you, that's all.'

'Well, I'm honoured.' He catches my eye. 'I'm also a bit worried about you.'

'Don't be.'

'I was glad to get your text. Next time, please can you get in touch sooner, though? I was already starting to worry.'

'Of course – sorry. I was out with Arthur and we lost track of time.'

In the kitchen, while I'm ordering (a 'Heaps of Meat' for Dad and a margherita with pineapple for me), I access the Guild's vehicle registration database. All agents have access to this system. I key in the number plate from our kidnappers' vehicle, 60N3 1R3, and wait . . .

'Do you want any sides with that?' asks the woman taking my order.

'Yes: please can we have garlic bread, wedges and chocolate-chip cookies, with cheese on everything?'

'You want cheese on the *cookies*?' She sounds horrified, but I'm busy staring at my phone. The database has finished its search for the number plate and has come up *No match*.

That isn't possible. I key the digits in again, but the same thing happens.

'If in doubt, add cheese,' I tell the woman at the pizzeria, distractedly. She names the amount to pay, and I recite the digits from Dad's card – I know the number off by heart.

As soon as I hang up the phone, I pull out my notebook and write down the registration number. There's something about it that's bothering me . . .

6ON3 1R3 . . .

Poirot's voice whispers in my ear: 'It is not much use being a detective, *ma petite*, unless . . .'

'Unless you are good at guessing,' I whisper to myself.

If the plate isn't registered on our system, someone must want to keep it that way. What secret is hiding in this number plate?

I stare at it until the numbers and letters reform as:

boNe iRe.

Bone ire? Why does that seem so familiar?

Another word for ire is *anger* or . . . *wrath*. So now I have *bone wrath* – or *Rathbone*!

I'm so excited, I don't even notice Dad's come into the kitchen until he speaks.

'You're looking very pleased with yourself. Did you just work something out for your case?'

I nod. 'I have to message someone.'

'Go on then. I'll sort the plates and drinks while you do that.'

'Thanks, Dad.'

I turn to go up to my room, but he calls after me, 'By the way, Aggie . . .'

I stop and look back. 'Yes?'

'I know you love your red coat, but you don't have to wear it in the house, you know.'

I glance down and take in that I've also not removed my boots.

'How did you get so filthy, anyway?' he asks.

I laugh. 'It's taken you a while to notice!'

'Hey! I pay attention!'

But he's blushing a little too. We both know he's not observant about appearance. (Unless you're a plant, in which case he can spot a greenfly on one of your leaves at ten paces.)

'Give it here – I'll brush it down for you,' he says.

I remove the dirty garment and hand it over. 'Thank you, Dad – I appreciate it.'

On the way upstairs, I start to shake. At first, I put it down to being a bit cold, but as the trembling gets more intense, I realise I'm in a minor state of shock. *Pull yourself together*, I tell myself sternly, gripping hold of the handrail alongside the stairs to my room. *Do you think Poirot allowed himself to fall apart at the slightest threat?*

Inside my attic haven, I sit on the bed and wrap my duvet round my shoulders before texting Arthur:

> 60N3 1R3 = Rathbone!!

His response comes almost immediately.

> Of course! Well done, Agatha. Proof at last!!

I frown and type back:

> But if this is his car, wouldn't his number plate appear on the registration database?

> Not if it's a forged plate that he switches with the real one, for his dodgy dealings

> I guess. But who uses a personalised number plate that can easily be traced back to them for criminal activities? You'd have to be an idiot

Maybe he is. We'll have to ask him tomorrow. Unless you think we should go over there now?

To ask if he's an idiot?

Among other things

I don't feel good about this

I know it's hard for you, because you're at school with his daughter, so you feel responsible. (Even if she is a nightmare, from what you've told me.) But it's looking pretty open and shut, don't you think?

I still can't help thinking about how she'll react once all this comes out. And what if we've made a mistake and it isn't Rathbone?

I refer you to the facts:
1. He's been closely involved with at least two paintings that are known to be forgeries (*Sunflowers* and *The Marriage*).
2. We were kidnapped pretty much immediately after confronting him.
3. He owns the car that was used to kidnap us today.
4. I've got a gut feeling. (I have a very reliable gut.)

I can't help laughing at that last one.

So the net is closing around Rathbone. And if he did have something to do with Mum's death, then he will certainly deserve a long prison sentence.

After I've finished messaging Arthur, I use my mobile to call Sam Cohen. His phone goes straight to voicemail. I decide against leaving a message, just in case his mystery visitor is still around.

I have two messages from Brianna on our group chat app.

Brianna
Bonjour, mon amie. Comment ça va avec your investigation? You are *manqu*ing to us. We are envious of your *nouveau ami*

I flinch at her awful franglais. She's followed this up with:

> **Brianna**
> How did you get out of school today? Any leads found or are you still searching?

> Still searching

Liam puts in:

> **Liam**
> What's easy to open but hard to close?

I think of replying 'A case', but instead I type:

> Your mouth?

He fills the screen with laughing emojis. I'm pretty sure they're meant sarcastically.

12.

A SNAKE IN THE GRASS

I try Sam Cohen again. He answers on my first ring.

'Hello. Who is it?' He sounds panicky.

'Mr Cohen, hi. Sorry to bother you. It's Agatha Oddlow – Clara's daughter.'

'No. Can't talk.' He hangs up the phone.

I sit staring at my mobile for a few seconds, wondering what on earth is going on. Then I run downstairs to the kitchen and use the landline to call him again, so he won't recognise my number.

He picks up immediately. 'Yes?'

I disguise my voice, deepening it and adding a hint of upper-class drawl.

'Hell-*ooo*. Is that the art conservator? My name is Lady Valerie DuBois. I was hoping you could help me with a painting I've been left in my mother's will.'

'Yes, of course, madam. I'm a little tied up right now, but if you could send me the details in an email—'

'Oh no!' I force a little laugh. 'I don't do modern technology, I'm afraid . . .'

'Right, well, if you give me your phone number . . .'

'Perhaps I could pop round with it? I'm going out at seven, and I could drop in on my way . . .'

'No!' There's no denying the panic in his tone.

'Very well. I shan't trouble you further today. I shall call again, to arrange a convenient time to discuss my mother's painting.'

'Thank you, Lady Valerie. I look forward to it. My apologies, but I must get on this evening.'

He hangs up without even saying goodbye.

So Sam Cohen is definitely in trouble of some kind. Yet he answered his phone. I wonder whether his mystery visitor has instructed him to wait by the phone for an important call. Perhaps Lord Rathbone has somehow discovered I'm in touch with the art conservator and is pressuring him into dropping his investigations into the forgeries.

Within less than a minute, I've made up my mind – I need to pay Mr Cohen a visit. It's the only way to find out what exactly is going on and if he's in danger.

I consider calling Arthur, but then I remember the state he was in on our way home earlier. He's in no condition to be back-up for an evening operation. Liam and Brianna? I check the time. It's quarter to seven. Should I involve my friends? As I sit on the bed deliberating, I hear my dad shouting from downstairs.

'Din-ner!'

Of course – the pizza! I haven't had anything since the hot chocolate at the Guild HQ, and I realise I'm starving. My stomach gurgles as if it's only just noticed how empty it is.

'Coming!' I shout.

I race downstairs, nearly running into Dad as I enter the kitchen.

'Hey! Slow down!' He laughs. 'Your pizza isn't going anywhere.'

'Sorry! I'm just really hungry.'

'Did you get any lunch?'

I shake my head. 'Not really.'

'You have to eat, Aggie!'

'Sorry, Dad.' I pause, wondering how he's going to react to my request.

'Dad . . .'

He sets two glasses on the table and looks at me. 'Yes?'

'Do you think . . .' I take a deep breath. 'Would you mind if I took this away?'

'Up to your room, do you mean?'

I shake my head. No – I mean out. 'I've just realised there's a place I need to visit, to check something out.'

'Right . . .' He sits down heavily on a chair at the table. 'I don't know if you're aware of this, but it's not always easy being your dad.'

I smile ruefully. 'Yeah, I know.'

'You do?'

I nod. 'You don't know whether to allow me the freedom I need to investigate things, or whether that makes you a negligent parent.'

'You do get it!'

'Of course. But you don't need to worry, Dad – I'm only going to visit an art conservator, not the lair of an evil mastermind.'

'A conservator?' I nod. 'Well, that sounds safe enough . . . And you'll take a taxi both ways?'

'Sure.' He gets up and fetches money from his wallet, which he hands to me. 'For your fare.'

'Thanks, Dad,' I say, taking it.

'And you'll be careful?'

I give him a kiss on the cheek. 'Always,' I promise.

'You'll need your coat.' He gestures to the back of the kitchen door, where my lovely red garment is hanging on the apron hook. All trace of the dirt and dust from the barn is gone.

'You got it clean! Thanks so much, Dad.'

'You're very welcome.'

He's scrutinising the top of my head. 'Shame I didn't get you to hand over your beret.'

I touch my beloved red hat. 'I forgot I was wearing it!'

'It's filthy.'

I pull a face. 'Maybe I can give it a brush before I go.'

He holds out a hand. 'Give it to me. I'll wipe it over while you grab everything you need.'

'Did I tell you I love you?'

He grins. 'That's cupboard love. But I'll take it.'

Sam Cohen lives in a tiny cottage in east London, not far from Bethnal Green station. The house is so old the whole of the black-and-white structure is wonky, where the timber and plaster have shrunk or swollen over the years. It's flanked by tall, shiny office buildings from the twenty-first century. This is another time when the word *incongruous* appears in my head. But which is out of place – the ancient cottage or the modern architecture? I'm guessing that depends on your outlook.

I don't knock on the door, but check for onlookers before skirting the building, searching for signs of forced entry. The windows all seem intact at the front and side. Access to the back of the house is via a high wooden gate, but this is locked. It looks as though anyone intimidating Mr Cohen must have knocked on the front door, like a civilised visitor.

I use my lock-picking kit to open the padlock and pass through the gate. A light is shining out on the ground floor. I creep over to the window, crouching low to keep from being spotted. There's a gap between the curtains, and I peer in.

I'm looking in at a little kitchen, where a man with dark but grey-flecked hair is sitting at a round table, with his head in his hands. I'm guessing this is the conservator himself. There's no sign of anyone else. The phone is next to his hand, as though he's expecting a call at any minute. When it rings, I nearly jump. I hadn't taken into account how old the windows are – there's no noise insulation in either direction. But this should work in my favour.

He answers the phone. 'Samuel Cohen.' There's a pause, then he says, 'I understand.'

It's frustrating, only hearing one side of the conversation.

'No, as I told when you called round, I haven't heard from Ms Oddlow's daughter. To be honest, I didn't realise she had a child.'

I am startled at hearing myself mentioned. So I was right: my contact with the art conservator is what's tipped off whoever's been menacing him. I was also right about him being a decent person – he seems to be protecting me. He looks so pale and fragile I feel a stab of guilt at having dragged him into all this.

He continues speaking. 'I'm sorry, I don't know that person either. Smith, you say? Where does she work? . . . Oh, I see. No, she never contacted me. Look, I really don't have anything you're looking for. I'm just going about my business. I'm really not sure what you want from me. If I hear from the daughter, I promise I'll notify you. No, I haven't forgotten . . .'

He's gone even paler and I could swear his hand

239

is shaking. When the call ends, he drops the phone as if it's burning his hand.

That's when he spots me. I've got so caught up with the scene inside, I've grown reckless. I'm pretty much staring straight at him through the window.

He leaps up. 'Who's there? I'm calling the police!'

But he does no such thing: he opens the back door and calls out. 'I know you're out there.'

'It's me, Agatha Oddlow,' I say quietly, walking towards him. 'I didn't mean to scare you.'

'I wondered if it might be you,' he says softly. He glances around the garden, checking there's nobody else about. 'You'd better come inside. It's freezing out here.'

I hadn't even noticed the temperature until he mentioned it. Now I realise soft flakes are falling, melting as they touch my coat.

I step inside, stamping my boots to disperse any dirt from the garden.

We're in the kitchen. There's a fireplace, but no fire is lit. Instead, Mr Cohen has an electric fan heater blowing. The air is warm and stuffy. He glances out of the window one last time, then hurriedly closes the gap in the curtains.

My host gestures for me to take a seat. 'Cup of tea?' he asks.

'No, thank you.' I remove my coat and beret, and place them over the back of a wooden chair before sitting down.

'If you'll excuse me, I'll just make one for myself . . .' He busies himself with the kettle, while I examine the room. I realise the table I'm sitting at is ancient and pockmarked with decades – centuries, even – of use by its many owners. The uneven white-plaster walls are decorated with paintings in ornate frames, and there are small sculptures and knick-knacks on every surface. It's like a miniature version of Sir John Soane's Museum.

I'm so busy examining my surroundings, it takes me a moment to realise Mr Cohen isn't making his tea. He's leaning against the deep trough sink, still holding the kettle, and shivering.

I get up and take the kettle from him. 'Sit down,' I tell him gently. 'I'll make your tea.' I pull out a chair and he takes a seat without a word. Glancing around, I see a blanket, folded over the back of an armchair in the corner. I take it and open it out, spreading the tartan wool throw over his shoulders. He clutches it round him, nodding to me gratefully.

I fill the black kettle and set it on the hob. There are matches alongside the old range cooker, and I light the gas and sit back down at the table, opposite the conservator.

'Are you all right?' I ask him.

'This . . . is . . . the first time I've been threatened,' he says slowly.

'And hopefully the last,' I say firmly. I take out my notebook. 'Now, what can you tell me about the person who threatened you? Was the phone call you just received from the same person?'

He nods, shuddering as he remembers. 'I recognised the voice.'

'Was it a man?'

He nods again. His shivering is slowing at last. 'Yes. He was tall – a lot taller than me.'

'About what? Five ten? Six foot?'

'A little over six foot. And big – broad-shouldered and heavy.'

I write this down. 'And can you describe his colouring?'

He shakes his head. 'They – he – was wearing a . . .' He draws a hand over his face.

'A balaclava?' I suggest.

'Yes! So I couldn't see his appearance. But there was something . . .' He grabs a jotting pad and makes a tiny, detailed drawing. I freeze as I see an elaborate letter A materialise on the paper. 'And he was wearing black-leather gloves.' He pauses, then says, 'I thought he'd come to kill me.'

'That must have been terrifying,' I say softly.

He nods. 'I've always felt safe here before. I've lived in this house for thirty-three years, and nobody has ever so much as shouted out an insult in the street. And now this . . .'

'The letter A,' I say. 'Where did you see it?'

'I saw it first on each of the fake paintings I tested.'

'That makes sense – I thought it must be a way of marking the forgeries.'

'It was also on the man's handkerchief.'

'His handkerchief?'

'Yes – I saw it when he got it out to mop under his balaclava, as if he was perspiring a lot. Normally, I would think it was just his initial, but it was identical to the one on the pictures.'

I study his sketch. There's no mistaking the similarity between this A and the one on the *Sunflowers* canvas.

'I'm so sorry,' I say, and he looks at me in surprise.

'Why are you sorry?'

I shrug. 'This didn't happen until I contacted you.'

'But you're not the one forging artwork. You're not sending thugs round to threaten innocent people.'

The kettle starts to whistle, and I get up and turn off the gas. There's a row of blue-and-white pottery mugs above the range, so I unhook one and take a teabag from the box on the side. As I place it in the mug and pour over the hot water, Mr Cohen says,

'Your mum was a brave woman, I think.'

'She was, wasn't she? I don't think I'd realised it until quite recently.'

'She was much braver than me.'

I turn back to him. 'You are very brave!'

'Me? You saw the state I got into, just from a phone call!'

'But you told the man you'd never heard of me – that you didn't even know I existed. That was incredibly courageous – you could so easily have told the truth.'

'You heard that?'

I nod.

'Well, I could tell from your voice over the phone that you were barely more than a child. I wasn't going to let them come after you.' He looks at me for a moment. 'Although, now I've met you, I sense there's rather more to you than I'd suspected. It must be because you're Ms Oddlow's daughter.'

'I'll take that as a compliment.'

'You should.'

I find a teaspoon in a drawer and fish out the teabag. The milk bottle is already out on the side, so I pour a little into the mug until the brew turns from golden brown to dark cream. Then I add a couple of heaped spoonfuls of sugar and stir until it's dissolved.

I place the mug in front of him. 'I've made it very sweet, for the shock,' I say.

'Thank you. You're very kind – just like your mother. I was so sad to hear she'd died.'

'Did you know her well?'

'Not at all. But she was always thoughtful in her dealings with me.'

'Didn't you suspect something bad might have happened to her, when you didn't hear from her again?'

'I always wondered . . . But she hadn't given me any contact details, beyond a postbox address. I searched for her, of course, but I was never able to track her down. The shop that had been handling the postbox addresses was replaced by a takeaway, so I couldn't find her through that. Eventually, I decided – or hoped – she must have finished the case and didn't need my input after all.'

'Can we talk some more about your visitor?' I ask.

'I can't tell you very much, as I said.'

'When did he come?'

'Quite soon after you and I spoke on the phone the first time, actually. I started work immediately, researching the current owner of O'Keeffe's *Lake George Reflection.*'

'What did you find out?'

'Not a lot, to be honest. It's the property of a private trust – they lend art to galleries and museums all over the world.'

'How did you find this out?'

'I placed a call. I have a friend at an archive that specialises in O'Keeffe's work. But I can't believe she'd be involved in anything shady.'

'No,' I say slowly. 'I don't think it had anything to do with her. Your visitor came too soon afterwards for that.'

A cold stone has appeared in my belly. I haven't felt this unsettled since . . . when? I reflect, and realise the last time was when I finally gained access to Mum's file in the Guild HQ – and the folder had been emptied.

How could anyone have found out about Sam Cohen's research into the possible forgeries? It's only been since Arthur and I began our investigation that he's attracted unwanted attention.

That's when I have to admit the unthinkable: *Arthur*.

I Change Channel and run through a list of question and answers. They appear before me, as if they've been written on a whiteboard:

Question: Who knew I'd communicated with Mr Cohen over Sunflowers and The Marriage – plus The Yellow House and Lake George Reflection?
Answer: Arthur.

Question: Who asked for the art conservator's name and immediately input it into his phone (or possibly even sent a text to a colleague)?
Answer: Arthur.

Question: Who gave me the cufflink and maintained Lord Rathbone was behind everything?
Answer: Arthur.

I stand up and pace the room. It isn't possible – is it? I Change Channel and replay scenes in my head: Arthur, joking with me the first time we met; Arthur, thanking me for saving his life.

'Are you all right?'

I'd forgotten that Mr Cohen was there!

'I'm sorry,' I say, stopping and meeting his gaze. 'I've just realised that someone I trusted has been betraying me – betraying us, because it looks as though he's passed on your name, and details of your involvement.'

'Are you sure it's them? Perhaps you're mistaken?'

'No, I don't think I am. It all makes sense, you see. He's the only person who had access to every part of the information.' But my head is still reeling, hoping to uncover another possibility.

It can't be him. I've trusted Arthur with my insecurities as well as my private hopes about getting justice for Mum. It occurs to me that I care too much about him, as a friend. He's become the person I'm closest to, after Dad, Liam and Brianna. Tears fill my eyes and I have to stop pacing, because I can't see.

'Don't forget that phones can be tapped, emails intercepted . . .' says Mr Cohen.

'I know. But some of this particular information was discussed face to face. So unless someone had planted a bug actually on him . . .' I sit down heavily. 'I don't want to believe it – I thought he was my friend . . .'

Mr Cohen regards me with an expression full of compassion. 'Do you need a cup of tea?' he asks.

I smile weakly. 'Thank you, but no. What I need to do is confront him.'

Sam Cohen's face creases up with concern. 'Please, don't take any chances. You didn't hear what he – what the visitor – said to me, the threats he made . . .'

'Don't worry. I'm used to dealing with bullies.'

'I didn't finish telling you about him,' he says.

I take a deep breath. 'You're right. What does his voice sound like?'

'Deep and northern – Liverpudlian or Geordie maybe. I'm afraid I'm not very good at accents.'

I make a note. 'OK. I'll ask my cheating colleague about him. There can't be too many of his associates that fit his build and accent. I'll make sure you don't get any more threats.'

But the conservator is reaching for his phone. 'There's no need for that . . .'

'Who are you calling?'

'The police. I've been a coward, not alerting them sooner. I can't let you put yourself in danger.'

'What do you mean, you've been a coward?'

He doesn't meet my gaze. 'Perhaps if I'd called the police when I first uncovered the fakes, your mother might still be alive.'

'What makes you think she didn't die naturally?'

'I'm sure of it,' he says. I meet his eye and wait. 'It was something the northern man said . . . What was it . . .? Ah, yes: "If you aren't straight with us, you'll go the same way as Clara Oddlow. You knew her, didn't you?"'

He sees me flinch and a look of distress crosses his face.

'I'm so sorry – how clumsy of me! You didn't know she'd not died naturally?'

'I suspected,' I say weakly.

'I assumed you knew . . .'

I did know. But it's still hard to hear someone say it out loud – it makes it real. I blink hard to stop the tears that are threatening to spill out. Mum was murdered. And by the sounds of it, she was definitely killed by the people behind the art forgeries. If I can catch them, I might be able to get justice for my mum. Hopefully, I'm not too late to help Sheila Smith too.

'I'm going to call the police,' he says again.

'Please don't – at least not until you've heard from me again.'

'All right. I'll give you a few days,' he says.

'Thank you. I just need a bit more time . . .' A final thought occurs to me. 'Do you know Sheila Smith?' I ask him.

'Yes, very well. She's a dear friend of mine. Why? Has something happened to her? That man asked about her too, but I was determined not to tell him anything that might implicate Sheila.'

'She's gone missing,' I say. 'And I think your blackmailer and my colleague might be behind her disappearance.'

He has a hand to his mouth in shock. 'Not Sheila! But she wouldn't hurt a fly!'

'I think she's still alive,' I tell him. 'I found proof that she's being held somewhere . . .' I don't want to lie to him, so I say no more.

'Poor Sheila!'

'I'm going to find her,' I say. 'It's going to be all right – I promise.'

He squeezes my hand as he shows me out of the back door. 'Don't take any risks,' he says. 'It isn't worth it.'

'I'll do my best,' I say.

As I head out to hail a cab, it occurs to me that Sam didn't even ask how I bypassed the lock on the gate. He really needs to step up his security. I keep glancing around, but there's no one watching as I make my way through the dark, sleeting streets to the main road.

13.

OUT WITH THE NEW, IN WITH THE OLD

Sitting in a black cab travelling home, I send a message to my dear, ever-reliable friends:

> I need you!

Liam replies instantly:

> **Liam**
> When and where?

> My house, in half an hour

> **Liam**
> As you know, my guardian doesn't like me going out after 8 on a school night, but I'll find a way to convince him!

> **Brianna**
> I'll get my brother to bring me. Need a lift, L?

> **Liam**
> Nah, it's fine, thanks – I'll take a taxi

I laugh, remembering that Liam accepted a lift once from Brianna's brother, and arrived at his destination green and shaken. He kept clutching my arm and saying, 'Never again!'

My friends are coming! I text Dad, to let him know I'm on my way home and that he's to expect visitors.

He texts back:

> Do I have to lay out the best china?

> Just the best crisps?

I decide to shelve thinking about Arthur's treachery until I'm back in the house, preferably with my real friends for support. However, while the rational part of my brain may have approved this plan, my emotions have another idea: anger is coursing through me like adrenaline.

I'm starting to doubt everything I've learnt about him – his near-photographic memory, his knowledge of art history and technique, his irreverent manner . . . Everything he ever said to me – and every accompanying expression – flashes up in my mind as the cunning concealment of a master of disguise. But why? I can't work out what his motives might be.

Whatever his reasons, I've been gullible and naive. Did my experience with Wallace Jones teach me nothing?

So, I think, *what is real?* Is Arthur's Auto-Focus mechanism merely an invention, to convince me we had things in common? And I fell for it too. Was I really so desperate to believe I wasn't alone in my quirky ways, that I accepted without question this packaged version of a friend and fellow investigator?

It was all vanity, I think to myself. *You looked at Arthur and it was like looking in a mirror.*

This time, the house is bright and welcoming as the taxi pulls up. I can see that Dad's made a fire in the living-room grate and he's sitting watching television.

It's only as I open the front door that I remember Professor D'Oliveira. *She doesn't know what I know about Arthur!* There isn't time to speak to her before my friends arrive, so I pull out my phone, switch it on and send her a message:

> Do <u>not</u> trust Arthur Fitzwilliam –
> I'll explain tomorrow

My phone rings almost immediately. 'Hello?' I say.

'What on earth was that message?' asks the professor's voice. 'You cannot just send a note like that, without any explanation.'

'Sorry. I just . . .'

Dad comes out of the living room, and I gesture to my mobile. He nods and retreats, closing the door behind him.

Opening the door to the stairs, I perch on the third step.

'Well?' says the professor.

'Is it safe to say here?'

'Our phone network is encrypted,' she says impatiently.

'Right . . . well . . .' and I fill her in on the order of events, followed by my reasoning. She goes very, very quiet. Eventually, I say, 'Professor?' just to check we haven't been cut off.

'I'm still here, child. I just . . . Of all the people . . .'

'I know. I feel like an idiot. I trusted him completely.'

'You will both have to be suspended, obviously.'

Panic grabs me by the tongue. 'Both?'

'Well, this is all hearsay. You can't expect me to believe your story, purely because you've spoken to me first. For all I know, Mr Fitzwilliam may have a similar story about you.'

'He doesn't.'

'So you say. But you must remember that one of our longest-serving and most-trusted staff members,

Wallace Jones, turned out to be a traitor. I can't take any more risks.'

I blink back tears. 'You can't honestly think . . . You must know . . .' My voice breaks. I can't believe the professor would suspect *me* – I'm the one who brought in Jones, after all.

There's a knock on the front door, and I come out from the stairs to open it. Brianna's on the doorstep, and I give her a one-armed hug while keeping the mobile pressed to my ear.

'Liam's just arriving,' she whispers, and I nod and keep the door open until he joins us, dressed in a beige wool overcoat and looking a little too grown-up somehow.

'What's wrong?' he whispers, and I put a finger to my lips before saying into my phone,

'You can't really think I'd—'

'I would like you to come in to see me at eight thirty tomorrow morning,' she says firmly. 'You'll be handing over your case to Sofia Solokov, who has finished the investigation she was conducting.'

Of course she has.

'But we have to find Sheila by the end of the day tomorrow,' I start. 'There won't be enough time for Sofia to catch up . . .'

'This is not open to discussion.'

I want to shout that it's not fair, but I know better than to continue to argue with Professor D'Oliveira. Perhaps she'll let me defend myself tomorrow, when we meet.

'Goodnight, Agatha,' she says. 'You did the right thing, coming to me.'

Then why does it feel as if I'm being punished?

'Goodnight, Professor,' I say dully.

As soon as Dad realises my friends have arrived, he very kindly vacates the living room. He even comes back bearing a tray with glasses, a bottle of coke and a big bowl of crisps, then creeps back out.

The three of us sit down and I gaze at my friends fondly. Right now, I feel so grateful to have Liam and

Brianna in my life. It feels like it's been a lot longer than a day since I last saw them.

'What did Hargrave say when he saw you were bald?' I ask Brianna, who has had her entire head shaved since yesterday morning.

She makes an impatient gesture. 'Tsk, who cares about that! What's going on with *you*?'

Liam leans forward. 'It's that Arthur guy, isn't it?'

'How did you know?' I ask.

He shrugs. 'I didn't like the sound of him.'

Brianna winks at me and whispers, 'Jealous, much?'

I don't respond to her jokey manner. 'Liam was right,' I say.

'I knew it!' he says with glee. Then he sees my expression and says, 'I don't mean . . . I mean . . . I'm just glad my instincts were right.'

'I wish mine had been,' I say glumly.

'Come on, then – what's he done?' asks Liam.

I tell them everything – about Sheila's disappearance, and the hieroglyphic symbols she used, about the forged paintings and the cufflink, and ending with our suspicions about Lord Rathbone.

'As soon as I started to look into the forgeries,' I say, 'Arthur began to steer me towards him as the likely culprit.'

'Sarah's dad's pretty annoying, but he'd never get involved in something like that,' says Brianna. 'He's far too worried about his reputation to think about breaking the law.'

'But you know he's been arrested, right?' says Liam.

'What?' I look at him in horror.

'You didn't know? It came up in my news feed on the way over here.' He taps on his phone and hands it over to me.

Renowned Millionaire Philanthropist
Arrested Over Stolen Paintings

Lord William De'Ath Rathbone was arrested this evening, amid claims he knowingly traded in stolen artworks. It is alleged that the peer, a well-known patron of the arts, is involved in a forgery ring believed to have been replacing famous paintings with forged copies. Police have refused to disclose details of the stolen artworks, but their value is rumoured to total millions. Lord Rathbone has made no comment on the charges he faces.

I hand the phone back to Liam.

'So who told the police about him?' he asks.

'I'm guessing it was Arthur,' I say. 'It's in his interests to find a scapegoat for his own crimes.'

'What are his crimes?' asks Brianna.

'I think it's bad. I'm pretty sure he's involved somehow in Sheila Smith's disappearance. And as I've worked out she was on to the forgers, I'm guessing that means Arthur's also involved with them.'

'So it's all one big interconnected web?' says Liam.

'Yes. Basically, Sheila must have accused someone of producing the forgeries – or perhaps she told the wrong person what she'd uncovered, expecting them to back her up. Instead, she was seized, probably on her way home from the local shops after work on Friday last week.'

'You seem pretty sure about all this,' says Brianna.

'Well, I was abducted myself,' I say, 'and while Arthur and I were locked in the barn—'

'Wait!' Liam interrupts. 'You were *abducted*? So, what – you were just going to leave that bit out?'

'I'm telling you now, aren't I? Anyway, the people who kidnapped us warned us off continuing the investigation. But what if Arthur knew them all along? What if the whole thing was a charade for my benefit?' I think back to the kidnapping. It feels like it happened days ago. Was it really only this afternoon?

We all go quiet for a moment. Then Liam says, 'Agatha, I think you should call Arthur.'

Brianna frowns. 'What? Why?'

'Because if she calls him, she can keep up the pretence of not knowing he's a double agent – and he might accidentally give more away. The moment she confronts him with this, he'll clam up and she might not be able to find out enough to help Sheila.'

'The boy makes sense,' says Brianna.

I check my watch. It's half past eight. 'I'll call him now.'

My friends come to stand on either side of me as I call Arthur.

'Hi, Aggie! How are you doing?'

'Not too bad, thanks. Are you over the shock from earlier?'

'Yeah. I reckon so. Sorry if I went pathetic on you.'

'No, you were fine. You'd been through something awful. Look, I was wondering – have you seen the news?'

'No, I've just got up. I went to bed when I got in. Why?'

'It's Rathbone. He's been arrested.'

'Really? Hold on – let me turn on my telly . . .' He's quiet for a moment, then I hear a television come on in the background. 'I love 24-hour news channels,' he says. There's another pause, and then he whistles.

'You've seen?' I ask him.

'Arrested on suspicion of trading in stolen art,' he says.

'So who do you think reported him?' I ask.

'I've no idea. Maybe the police have been monitoring his dealings.'

'I wasn't even sure it was Rathbone behind all this.'

'I know! But I think they've got the right guy,' he says.

'I hope you're right, especially as they've released his name. It'd be pretty awful if he's innocent.' I pause. 'And we still don't know what's happened to Sheila,' I say quietly.

'*Only fourteen hours to save the Earth,*' he says in a cheesy voice.

'No, actually it's more like twenty-four.'

'It's a *Flash Gordon* quote,' whispers Liam in my ear.

Even so, *twenty-four hours*. How can I possibly find Sheila and rescue her in that time – especially as I have to report to Professor D'Oliveira at eight thirty in the morning? I decide to ignore the fact she's taken me off the case. After all, it's never stopped me before.

I finish the call to Arthur, promising to text him in the morning. Then I turn to my friends.

'We have got to find Sheila *now*,' I say. 'Liam, is there any way to trace an unlisted vehicle registration number?'

'I can find most things,' he says.

I kiss his cheek. 'Thank you!'

'What's my job?' asks Brianna.

I reflect for a moment. 'You're helping me,' I say.

14.

THE SPACE ABOVE

Dad calls Liam's guardian to ask his permission for Liam to spend the night. We hear Dad saying, 'No trouble at all. Yes – he can have the sofa.'

Then it's Brianna's turn. This just involves texting her brother to say she won't be home. 'Oh – the seniors are away again,' she tells us. That's what she calls her parents.

'Do they *ever* come home?' I ask her.

'Not if there's champagne and tennis, and preferably a yacht, available somewhere else.'

'I'm going to get on to the vehicle registration search,' says Liam. 'Can I use your computer?'

'Of course.' Brianna and I follow him upstairs to my room. While he's tapping in codes and calling up screens of script, Bri and I sit on the bed, and I show her the letter from Mr Cohen, the art curator.

'So your mum knew about the forged art?'

'Yes. It's what got her killed.'

'You really think she was murdered? I mean, I know you've wondered before now . . .'

I repeat what Mr Cohen told me – the threat about going 'the same way as Clara Oddlow'.

Brianna takes my hand and squeezes it. 'That must have been tough to hear.'

Tears start brimming in my eyes again.

'We're going to catch them, Aggie,' she says gently.

Then she immediately becomes brisk and businesslike, to give me a chance to pull myself together.

'Now, I've been thinking – what if your mum had other notes stashed away? I mean, she did a pretty thorough job of hiding this letter. Do you think she could have concealed details of other investigations in a similar way?'

Simultaneously, we both look at my bookshelves.

'She wouldn't have done anything to damage the Agatha Christies,' I say, ruling out two whole shelves of books.

'So it would have to be a book – or books – with little or no sentimental value. How about this?' She draws out a hardback volume on blood-spatter patterns.

I shake my head. 'Nope. That one's mine.'

'Of course it is,' she says drily. 'I bet it's your bedtime reading.'

'How about this one?' I pull out an art book I've never studied in detail. It's called *Neue Sachlichkeit* and has an ugly picture of a naked man and woman on the front. The text is all in German, which is why – combined with the off-putting cover image – I've never spent time looking at it.

'Go on,' she says.

I turn to the back and – *yes!* – I feel a bulge inside the cover, just like the one I found in the *Story of Art* book. My hand is shaking as I take my penknife and gently slice apart the layers.

Inside, I can see the corners of some lined paper. I draw it out and unfold it. There's just one sheet, and it bears my mum's neat writing in purple ink. I'd forgotten how she liked to use coloured pens – she said they brightened the world.

My eyes blur with tears, and I have to blink hard to clear them. I'm holding another piece of Mum. That's what it feels like – as if I'm slowly fitting her back together, from the pieces she left behind.

Brianna is at my elbow. 'What does it say?'

There are letters on the paper, but they don't form words:

yuu'kl ib wkp qnoc's glsh
exe hdexe bʒ shlow glaie tiojh bʒi

I'm filled with frustration. 'It's in code!'

'So?' says Brianna. 'Aren't you an ace codebreaker?'

'It's not something you just do in half a minute. And if this is Mum's code, it's bound to be a tough one.'

'Except you're her daughter, don't forget. If anyone knows how her mind worked, it's you.'

'I was seven when she died,' I protest.

'Maybe we can work it out together,' she suggests.

So I place the page on the bed and Brianna and I kneel side by side on the floor, staring at the letters.

'How would you normally start?' asks Brianna.

'I'd look for a repeating set of three letters, which will usually represent "the". That'll give us the letters T, H and – most usefully – E. Then we need to find a single letter that repeats frequently – that's likely to be A.

'Hmm, makes sense,' says Brianna. 'Could it just be one of those shift codes? You know, the ones where the whole alphabet has shifted two letters to the left or something?'

'That just seems too basic for Mum,' I say. I gaze at the page. 'There's not enough here to find a pattern!' It's true: it's only a short message, with only a few characters.

I close my eyes and Change Channel, bringing up memories of Mum from all those years ago. She's calling 'Hello, house!' as she opens the front door. She's laughing as she freewheels down the hill on her bike, with me strapped in a seat behind her and shouting out with excitement. She's in the swimming pool, teaching me breast stroke. She's handing me a lock-picking kit and waiting patiently while I tackle my first padlock. She's sitting on the chair beside my bed, a book open on her lap, reading me stories of criminals and the great detectives who thwart them.

When I open my eyes, the cipher has shifted into focus.

'I'm the key,' I say.

'What do you mean?' asks Brianna.

'It's a Vigenère cipher and my name's the key – *Agatha Oddlow*.'

'Does that mean the message is only made up of the letters in your name?'

I shake my head. 'No – it works on polyalphabetic substitution.'

She raises an eyebrow. 'Of course it does.'

'Look.' I write 'AGATHA ODDLOW' at the top of a page in my notebook. Now I write out the letters of the alphabet beneath my name. 'So you see how the first A of "Agatha" lines up with A at the start of the alphabet, but the G of "Agatha" corresponds to B, the second A to C, the T to D, and so on?'

'Yep. Is that it?' She sounds disappointed.

I shake my head. 'It's like a double layer of concealment. The new letters then get allocated a whole other set of characters in a grid. Without the key, it can be a nightmare to decode.'

I feel a familiar buzz of excitement as I set to work on deciphering Mum's code.

It's fairly quick work now I know the key. *'You're in the crow's nest . . .'* I say. 'That's what Mum called my bedroom!'

'Brilliant!' says Brianna. 'So, "You're in the crow's nest" . . .?'

'But there is still . . .'

'Still what?' asks Brianna. 'What is there, above the crow's nest?' she muses. 'Isn't the whole point that it's at the top of the boat, the top of the world?'

'Sky?' I suggest, though that's too short for the letters in the message.

We look at each other and say in unison, *'Space!'*

I decode the word to check it. 'Yes – *space*, that's right.'

I go quiet again while I work out the remaining part of the message.

At last, I sit back and read: *'You're in the crow's nest but there is still space above you.'*

Brianna frowns. 'What does that mean?'

'The loft hatch outside my bedroom!' I say. 'It leads to a tiny storage space!'

We have a full-size loft, which we can access from Dad's room. It's filled with damaged goods: three-legged chairs and other broken or cast-off furniture and toys. The 'loft' outside my room, on the other hand, is a very small rectangular space. I remember Mum showing it to me once, but it never occurred to me she might have had an ulterior motive. What was it she said . . .?

I close my eyes as I recall her words.

'"*This is a good place if you ever need to hide something small.*"'

15.

WILL THE REAL ARTHUR FITZWILLIAM PLEASE STAND UP?

Brianna and I walk out on to the landing and look up at the wooden board that serves as a door to the little space.

'Do you have a ladder?' she asks.

'Yeah – I think there's one in a cupboard down in Dad's room.'

Dad's downstairs watching telly, so it's easy to fetch the wooden ladder from his room without having to answer any questions. I struggle a bit with manoeuvring the steps along the landing and up the narrow stairs to the second floor. 'Ouch!' I shout, as I graze my knuckles on the wall.

'Are you all right?' calls Brianna, who's waiting at the top of my stairs. She helps me to position the ladder, and we use it to try and push open the hatch. But it won't budge.

'It must be locked,' she says.

I grab my head torch and put it on. 'Hold the ladder,' I say, as I start climbing to the top. Up close, I examine the hatch and, sure enough, there's a keyhole. The shape of it reminds me of the key I wear round my neck . . . I draw it out and fit it into the lock. It's a little stiff when I go to turn it, but after a moment there's a satisfying *click* and I'm able to push the wooden hatch open.

Clouds of dust and cobwebs come tumbling down. Brianna jumps back quickly, but I get covered in filth. I have to wait until the air clears before I can see properly again.

'You OK up there?' she asks.

I'm not sure how to answer. There's a heavy feeling in my stomach, which is getting worse the closer I come to finding out what Mum has left for me to find. What if it's something disturbing or upsetting? Or what if I've misinterpreted the code, and there's nothing up here at all? I can't decide which option would be worse. My palms are damp and slippery, so I wipe them on my dress.

'Ready?' asks Brianna, when the dust has settled.

Let it be something nice, I think to myself as I step up the last two rungs until I can see inside the dark opening.

The loft space is even smaller than I remembered – my torch easily lights the whole area – but it's packed with small items. I can see several shoeboxes, a hatbox, a small suitcase, a video, a Thermos flask and a box of Lego. I reach in and rummage around, exposing an old DVD player, two biscuit tins, a moth-eaten coat, a jigsaw and a video. A *video*? I draw it towards me. The writing on the front announces that it contains the first three episodes of the TV series of *Agatha Christie's Poirot*. One final glance around confirms this must be the object I'm meant to find.

I grab the small box and gingerly climb back down.

I'm glad I've got Brianna there, holding the ladder steady – but I'm still relieved when I can jump down from the third step to the landing. Leaving the steps where they are, we hurry back into my bedroom and open the box. There's just a VHS tape inside.

Liam joins us and we stand in a row, staring at the black rectangle of plastic.

'What is it?' asks Brianna.

'A VHS tape,' says Liam. When Brianna continues to look blank, he adds, 'A video.'

'Oh – why didn't you say so? But . . . do you even own a video player, Aggie?'

'I don't think so,' I say.

Brianna picks it up and shakes it. 'Do they normally rattle like this?' she asks.

'No,' I say.

'Definitely not,' agrees Liam.

We peer over her shoulder to inspect the two tape spools that should be visible inside the transparent part of the casing. But they're not there.

'This is some weird video. Shall I open it?' asks Brianna.

Liam and I both nod, and she prises the plastic apart. Inside, there's a DVD.

I feel a bit like I'm at a kids' party, playing pass-the-parcel – each layer I unwrap just leads me to another inexplicable package.

'Hopefully, it won't just come up with a self-deleting warning,' I say. Then I remember I haven't told them about the memory stick yet. 'Oh – I'll explain later.'

Liam inserts the CD into my computer and we wait. Liam sits in the chair and Brianna perches on the arm, but I'm too on edge to sit down, so I pace.

Within a few seconds, it starts playing, and I feel as if I've been punched in the ribs – because there's Mum, looking straight at me. I turn up the volume. And then her voice comes out, as clear as when she was alive:

'If you're watching this, my darling Agatha, it means you've turned into a great codebreaker, just like I knew you would.' She pauses and when she speaks again, her tone is soft and sad: 'It also means I've died . . . Please believe me, when I say I would never have chosen to leave you – and I certainly won't have gone without a fight. I love you, sweet-heart. Never doubt that.'

A drop of water falls on my hand. When did I start crying? Brianna and Liam – I'd forgotten they were here – come to stand on either side of me.

'I don't have long,' says Mum. 'I need to share with you what I've discovered. But if I've gone, then it's likely that my current investigation is what sealed my fate. Anything I tell you may put you in danger, my darling. For my sake – please, please don't do anything reckless.

'First of all, there's a woman you need to seek out. She's called Professor Dorothy D'Oliveira, and you can track her down at the Royal Geographical Society, where she's a senior fellow in hydrology. She will be able to advise and protect you.'

(*Oh, Mum!* I think. *This advice is coming a bit late!* It's both distressing and wonderful to have my mum talking to me like this, but I hope there's going to be something really useful in what she says, to help us find Sheila.)

'As I said,' Mum continues, 'I don't have long – I'm

pretty sure there's someone coming after me – so I'll get straight to the point. I've been investigating an organisation who call themselves "The Alumni". It began as a group of ex-students, all from the same school, but they've expanded since. The group's mission is to acquire works of art by top artists, because they believe, arrogantly, that they are the only people who can truly appreciate them. They are willing to use any means necessary to source and obtain the artworks.

'The main line of my investigation has been a forgery ring. I believe that, for a number of years now, agents of the Alumni have been stealing world-famous paintings and replacing them with forgeries. However, they are very clever at covering their tracks. For instance, although I have established links with several major international galleries, I still don't know who is at the head of the forgery operation. Goodness knows how many thefts have taken place altogether. The Alumni get other people to carry out the thefts for them, and are careful never to expose their main operatives.'

She pauses.

Then she says, 'These people will stop at nothing to get what they want. Seek the professor's help – and keep safe, my darling. Remember that I love you.'

The screen goes black. I wait, but there's nothing more.

'Wow, are you OK?' asks Brianna.

I shrug, fairly sure I'll break down if I try to talk. I feel as if I've just got Mum back – as if someone's shown her to me, only to take her away again.

Liam and Brianna put their arms round me and we have a big hug.

'The A on the *Sunflowers* painting . . .' I say.

'A for Alumni,' says Brianna, and I nod.

'But if the Silver Serpent doesn't refer to Lord Rathbone,' I say, 'then who or what does it refer to? Of course! I should have realised the snake on the Rathbone crest was nothing like the one on Sheila's letter . . .' I see their bewildered faces and realise this is another detail they know nothing about. 'Remind me to keep you in the loop with my investigations in future,' I tell them.

'Yes, please do,' says Brianna.

'Are you feeling better now, though?' asks Liam, and when I nod, he adds, 'Good – because I've traced that registration number.'

'Really?' I say.

'Yep. It took me ages.'

'It's been less than an hour,' says Brianna drily.

'Well, it felt like ages,' he says.

'So?' I ask him. 'Who's the car registered to?'

'Someone I've never heard of – a Tabitha Fitzwilliam?'

There it is, the proof I needed. *Fitzwilliam*. Even though I was pretty sure that, all along, Arthur had been working against me – against the Guild, I still feel a shiver along my arms and back.

'Fitzwilliam?' I say, 'Are you sure?'

He nods. 'Quite sure.'

'That's Arthur's surname,' I tell them.

They look at each other and then at me.

'So he's not just an Alumni henchman – it's his own nefarious scheme,' says Liam. 'I've always wanted an opportunity to use that word.'

'"Nefarious" is a great word,' I say. 'But I'm

guessing Tabitha Fitzwilliam is his mum, so we don't know if it's his plan or hers. In fact, it's possible they're both working for someone else. More importantly, this means Sarah's dad had nothing to do with the kidnapping – they were just trying to frame him. He probably doesn't know anything about the forgeries either.'

'Do you still want to play along with Arthur?' asks Brianna. 'Only, I feel a confrontation might be in order, now we know he was in on the kidnapping as well.'

'I want to find out what they did to my mum,' I say.

'I'm definitely up for it,' says Liam. 'I'd like to tell this Arthur what I think of anyone who treats my friend Aggie badly.'

'Where does he live?' asks Brianna.

I shake my head. 'I just know it's near Greenwich, because of what he said to the taxi driver, but I don't even know if that's true.'

'Ah, but I have an address,' says Liam triumphantly. 'They hadn't covered their tracks as well as they thought. I tracked down the online shop that they'd ordered the false number plate from, and was able to hack their customer records. The address was listed: The Lodge, Greenwich Park. As it's in Greenwich, I bet it's the right one.'

'You really are amazing,' I tell him, and he grins with pride.

'It's ten o'clock already. Are you two sure about this?' I ask them.

'Definitely,' they say in unison, and grin.

We leave by my trusty old escape route of the skylight and the oak tree. Liam and Brianna clearly find the whole climbing-on-to-the-roof-and-leaning-across-to-grab-a-tree experience a bit too thrilling. There's a lot of shrieking and laughter.

'*Shhh!*' I tell them. 'Dad might hear.' We can't risk him trying to stop us from going. He might just about have adjusted to the idea that *I* sometimes have to take off at strange hours – but he's bound to feel responsible for my friends' welfare, while they're staying with us.

Once we're on the ground, we duck and run, until we're out of sight of the house. Then we hasten through the park to Park Lane and hail a black cab at Marble Arch.

I don't have a plan as we sit in the taxi and watch the meter piling on the pounds. It seems pointless to even attempt to prepare for an encounter with someone it turns out I know nothing about. My 'friend' has proved as fake as the combined forgeries of *The Marriage*, *Sunflowers* and *The Yellow House*. Was anything he told me true? I wonder, not for the first time: *who is the real Arthur Fitzwilliam?*

It was dark when we set out, but by the time we arrive, the clouds have parted enough to allow the full moon to shine through. The light illuminates a pair of grand metal gates, the sort that mark the entryway into the grounds of a mansion. Nothing about the Arthur I've met has led me to expect his home to be so grand.

I open the little window into the driver's cab. 'Are you sure this is right?' I say.

'The Lodge at Greenwich Park,' he says. 'This is it.'

'It's that little house there,' says Liam, pointing through the ornate scrollwork gates to a tiny flint cottage on the other side.

We climb out and I pay the driver and take a receipt. There's a sudden draught as a helicopter passes overhead, perhaps en route to or from the nearby Old Royal Naval College building.

As I stash away the receipt, I mutter, 'Maybe when I'm allowed back in the Guild, I'll be able to claim it back.'

'What?' says Liam. 'Agatha – have you been suspended *again*?'

'Yeah. I reported Arthur, and Professor D'Oliveira said she had to suspend both of us.'

'What?' says Liam. 'When were you planning on telling us?'

'After we solved everything . . .' I avoid meeting his eye.

'Do you reckon the professor's contacted him?' asks Brianna. 'Only we'd lose the element of surprise if he knows you're on to him.'

I shrug. 'I haven't got a clue. But he can't really be expecting me to turn up with both of you at quarter to eleven at night.'

'I hope not,' says Liam. 'I'm starting to wonder if we didn't really think this through. What if his parents are black belts in karate or something?'

'I'm wondering something else,' says Brianna.

'What?' we both ask.

'Why's there a helicopter landing in the park?'

We all look up. The helicopter I'd seen before is now hovering above us, its lights illuminating the little lodge house. There's a wind from the propellers – it's like standing under a giant fan. We duck instinctively.

'Someone's coming out of the house!' I say to the others, dragging them to the side, where thick hedging gives us cover.

We peer through the hedge and see the figure starting to flash a torch, apparently signalling to the pilot.

'It's Morse code,' I say. I count the long and short flashes. 'It's a short message: *Sil-ver Ser-pent.*'

Then the helicopter moves further away into the grounds, and we lose sight of it, although we can still hear its propellers whirring. The figure steps back inside the lodge – and, for a moment, he's up, and I see it's Arthur. *He's the Silver Serpent!*

'We need to get through these gates,' I whisper to my companions. I try the latch, but it's firmly locked. Then I put one foot on the metal scrollwork and discover it's easy to climb – the intricate pattern provides plenty of footholds.

I jump down on the other side and see my friends have both made it to the top. Liam jumps from quite high up and lands neatly. He has tennis coaching at least twice a week and all those lessons have clearly made him nimble. Brianna takes advantage of her long legs by stretching one foot to the ground and then swinging the other down to meet it.

We creep forward until we're level with the wall of the house. Then we freeze. The front door opens and Arthur is again framed in the light shining from inside. He steps out and is followed immediately by a tall, slim woman.

We scamper back towards the gate and make it in time – they don't spot us. I glance at my friends and see my own relief reflected in their faces. It seems strange that we're hiding from someone I would have trusted with my life until a few hours ago.

'Was that Arthur?' asks Liam.

I nod. 'The woman could be his mother, Tabitha.'

'So why are we hiding?' asks Brianna. 'I thought the plan was to confront them.'

'It is,' I say. 'But now I want to see what's in that helicopter, before we announce ourselves.'

They both nod.

As soon as Arthur and his mother have vanished into the park, we follow. Not that we need a guide – the helicopter's propellers are still turning, creating a vortex of wind and sound.

We approach it cautiously, ducking behind shrubs and trees, but the people milling round it are too involved in their business to notice us. The door has been slid back, and two figures on board are handing down large packages to Arthur and Tabitha, who stash each item on a trolley before returning to receive the next.

'What've they got?' says Brianna. 'Can you tell?'

Things are clicking into place in my mind. Files at the back of mind that have been half-open for several days, awaiting further information, are now closing.

'It's art,' I say slowly. 'I don't know if these are the original masterpieces or the forgeries, but those packages contain paintings – I'm sure of it.'

'I guess we know why he didn't want Sheila Smith sticking her nose in,' whispers Brianna.

16.

SECRETS AND LIES

We hear one of the helicopter crewmen ask, 'Is that everything for tonight?'

Tabitha replies, 'Yes – all done.'

The aircraft's door is closed and they take off. The current from the propeller grows strong and then slackens off as the lights recede into the dark sky.

Liam, Brianna and I keep out of sight as Arthur and his mother secure the goods – I count five large, picture-shaped packages – on the trolley and wheel them to the house. We follow at a safe distance and wait until they're in and the front door shuts behind them.

'Shall we knock or just burst in?' Liam asks.

'I'm not sure it's the kind of door you can burst in through,' says Brianna. We all look at the sturdy oak barrier, with its metal studs.

'We could try the handle . . .' Liam suggests.

'I'm going to knock,' I decide.

I rap on the door with the metal knocker. It sounds too loud in the night. As we wait in the cold and dark, I start to doubt the wisdom of our mission. Confronting Arthur seemed like such a good idea back in my bedroom – after all, wasn't I owed an explanation, and maybe even an apology? But now I'm acutely aware that it's just gone eleven o'clock on a winter's night and I've brought my friends to visit a pair of criminals.

We don't have to wait long before the door is opened by Arthur. In the light flooding out, he sees me and at least I have the satisfaction of watching the shock pass over his face before his habitual joviality returns.

'*Agatha* – is that you . . .? And your friends – Liam and, er, Brianna, is it? What on earth are you doing here?'

He raises an eyebrow and cocks his head on one side – an attitude I would have found charming only this morning. Tonight, it makes me angry.

'We're here because we know everything,' I say. 'You and your mum are working for the Alumni, stealing paintings and replacing them with forgeries.'

His face changes. It's as if someone has removed a mask. The twinkle and dimples give way to a calculating grimace. He's weighing up how much I know and how much I'm just guessing.

'You'd better come inside,' he snaps.

I glance at my friends. Neither of them looks enthusiastic. 'No, Arthur. I think it's better if we talk out here,' I say.

'Agatha, it's freezing!' he says. 'I'm not staying here with the door open.'

'It *is* pretty cold,' says Liam, rubbing his arms. 'Maybe it wouldn't do any harm to go in.'

So as we follow Arthur through the front door and into a small hallway, I say, 'I've told the professor what I've found out about you.'

'Have you now? And what is that exactly?' he asks

without turning to face me. The hall feels cold, with a tiled floor, and there are only two doors leading off it. He throws open the first and gestures for us to enter.

'After you,' I say, determined not to let him lock us in there.

'Fair enough.' He walks in and we troop in behind him.

We're in a square living room, also with a tiled floor, and with four high-back armchairs set in a semicircle facing a fire that's going out. A few embers still glow weakly in the grate, but there's no warmth coming from them.

I glance at Liam and Brianna and see I'm not the only one feeling less confident now we're on Arthur's territory. The balance of power has shifted and I'm not sure who's got control. This is definitely not how I'd imagined it. I'd thought in the taxi on the way over that I'd confront Arthur and his façade would crumble as soon as he admitted his guilt. He'd sob as he told me how bad he felt stringing me along and betraying not only me but the entire Gatekeepers' Guild.

'Was anything real?' I ask Arthur. 'I'm betting you don't really have the near-photographic memory or your so-called Auto-Focus mechanism . . .'

He shakes his head. 'No, Agatha, you're wrong. I do have those. It was amazing to meet someone else like me—'

'But not amazing enough to stop you betraying the Guild,' I say. My voice cracks, and I wish I had a better control of my emotions. I don't want to give him the satisfaction of seeing how much he's hurt me.

Just then, his mother appears in the doorway. She stops and looks from the three of us to Arthur.

'What on earth are *they* doing here in the middle of the night?' she asks.

'They've come to tell me *they know everything*,' he says.

I take in her bony figure, her dark hair with the purple streak and her piercing blue eyes.

'You're the attendant from Sir John Soane's Museum!' I say. 'The one who told me Lord Rathbone had sent *The Marriage* for cleaning. I'm pretty sure you're also Tabitha Fitzwilliam, Arthur's mother.'

'And you're that Agatha girl –' she puts on a silly, childish voice – '"Oh, can I see the famous paintings? Only, I have a school project due in tomorrow." As if!'

'Just tell us where Sheila Smith is, and we'll leave,' says Liam bravely.

Tabitha laughs. 'Do you really think you're in a position to make demands? You're in our house, on our property, and – I'm guessing – nobody knows you're here.'

She's right. We've walked straight in, like idiots. But I'm weighing the odds and I reckon that, if it comes to it, the three of us can easily take the pair of them. Even one-to-one, my own fighting skills are far superior to Arthur's.

'I've just sent a text,' I say. 'Someone will come.'

'Sorry, Agatha, but I know that's a lie,' says Arthur. 'I set up a signal blocker a few minutes ago, in case any locals tried to report the helicopter.'

'What? But that's illegal!' says Liam.

Arthur laughs. 'No! Is it really?'

That explains why he'd used Morse code to signal to the crew, I realise.

'You can stop all this now,' I tell him. 'Give yourself up, Arthur. You'll get a more lenient sentence.'

His mother laughs. 'He'll get an even more lenient sentence if he *doesn't* hand himself in!'

'Let's all sit down,' says Arthur, 'and talk about this.'

It seems ridiculous to sit down with them and act politely like we're guests, but I have no idea how long this is going to take. I look round at my friends, who nod their agreement, so we all sit.

'So let's start with what you're doing here,' says Arthur.

'Catching you in the act,' I say. 'We know you received paintings tonight. I bet they're forgeries, to replace the originals that you're going to help steal. Why are you doing this?'

Tabitha makes a snorting noise. 'And this from the girl who wouldn't know an authentic Hogarth from a copy.' I wait, but she doesn't bother saying any more.

I try working on Arthur again. 'You do realise, don't you, that what you're doing is illegal?'

'Who's it harming, exactly?' he asks.

Brianna sits forward. 'Er . . . the people who believe they're looking at genuine, original artwork. If you visit the Louvre to see the Mona Lisa, you expect to see the real deal.'

'If these people can't tell it's not the "real deal", they don't deserve to view the "real deal",' drawls Tabitha.

'And if even the art curators can't tell the difference, why does it matter?' asks Arthur.

'But the curators *can* tell the difference,' I say. 'That's why Sheila went missing, isn't it – because she knew something wasn't right. Where is she, Arthur? What have you done with her?'

'Sheila wouldn't stop asking questions,' he says. 'And now you're starting to be just as annoying as her.'

'Is that a threat?' asks Liam.

Arthur looks him in the eye. 'I was hoping to avoid this, but it might have to be.'

'I feel like such an idiot,' I say. 'I really thought you were a decent human being. A bit of a joker, maybe – but not a criminal.'

'I would direct my learned friend's attention to my previous question,' says Arthur, as if he's in a court of law. 'Who are we harming?'

I tick off the answers on my fingers: 'Well, apart from the fact that it's dishonest and deceitful, you're harming, specifically, Sheila Smith, Samuel Cohen – and *my mum*. There might be others I don't know about.'

'But fortunately for us,' says Arthur, 'you don't have proof of any of that—'

'But fortunately for *us*,' says Liam, cutting him off, 'the police are on their way. I found a way round your signal blocker.'

Arthur looks unsettled. I can tell he isn't sure if what Liam's claiming is possible.

I know Liam *is* bluffing – he keeps his expression poker-straight when he's lying, like now – but I love him for it. I wonder how I could have been hoodwinked by Arthur into thinking him a suitable friend. Liam and Brianna have bravery and principles running through them like the word *Blackpool* through a stick of rock.

'Hand me your phone,' he challenges Liam.

I stand up and step in front of my friend. 'You'll have to get past me first.'

'With pleasure,' says Arthur, rising to his feet.

I laugh. 'Really? Which one of us has martial arts training?'

Arthur jumps into the air, spins round, then lands on one leg, high-kicking the other. I can feel a breeze as the sole of his foot skims past my nose. 'You were saying?'

I'm rarely lost for words . . . I had been so sure I could beat him in a fight. At last, I manage, 'Where did you . . .?'

'Do you think Mr Zhang is the only martial arts *sifu* in the whole of London?'

Brianna gets up and comes towards me. 'Agatha, it's time to leave,' she says quietly. When I don't respond, she tries again, 'We have to go. Now.'

I'm still facing Arthur, sizing him up.

He says, 'You thought you could take me, didn't you?'

'How do you know I can't?'

He stands, one foot in front of the other, his hands raised and loose. He has the stance and confidence of someone who knows how to fight. Would I be able to beat him, if it came to it?

'Agatha – don't,' murmurs Liam, clearly reading my thoughts. 'We'd do better getting out of here. Leave him for the police.'

'OK, but there is one thing,' I say, still looking at Arthur. 'What can you tell me about my mum?'

The room goes very quiet. Arthur doesn't answer, but his mother steps towards me.

'What about your mum?' asks Tabitha after a moment. She sounds wary.

'Did you kill her?'

'You need to be very careful, making accusations like that,' she says.

'I know the Alumni murdered her because of her investigation. Did you have anything to do with it?'

'I know nothing about your mother, so I certainly didn't have a hand in her death,' she says coldly.

I sigh. Even if Tabitha does know something about Mum, she clearly isn't going to share it with me.

Frustration and disappointment flood in – but I can't let myself be taken over by negativity right now, when my friends need me. So gathering myself together and turning towards the door, I say firmly, 'You're right, Liam. It's time to leave.'

But Tabitha is in the way. We could get past her – but as I assess the route, Arthur steps alongside her. I don't fancy our chances against him. It's dawning on me – rather late – that they really might not be amenable to the idea of letting us leave and go home, not with the knowledge we have now. I catch Brianna's and Liam's eye, and see they're having similar thoughts. I look around and spot a landline telephone on the sideboard. Arthur may have blocked mobile signals, but the landline should still be working. It's close to where Brianna is standing. I give a faint nod of my head towards it and she nods slightly in return, to show she's understood.

I need to create a distraction, so addressing Arthur and his mother, I say, 'I bet you're wondering how we got here. Well, Liam's the one who traced the registration—'

'I thought you said that wouldn't be possible,' says Tabitha impatiently to Arthur. 'You said it was unlisted . . .'

'It shouldn't have been possible!' objects her son.

'Anything's possible online, if you know what you're doing,' says Liam, stepping forward. Arthur's eyes flick over Liam's neat frame, as if he's sizing him up as an opponent. My breathing grows more difficult at the thought of anyone hurting my friend. Liam is fit from all the tennis – but he's no trained fighter.

Then out of the corner of my eye, I see Brianna grab the phone. It's one of those that's just a handset, so it's fairly easy to be discreet. But she still needs to key in 999 – and then how will she speak, when someone answers?

Liam doesn't turn away from Arthur. The pair of them seem to be having a staring contest. I've never seen my former Guild partner stand so still – he's normally like a big puppy, full of energy and mischief. *No*, I remind myself – *you don't know what Arthur is 'normally' like.*

Each time I remember this, the pain is as sharp as the moment in Mr Cohen's kitchen when I realised Arthur was a traitor. It's almost inconceivable that he could hurt me in this way – that he could have been so scheming. Worst of all is the awareness that I've been fooled again. How does that saying go? *Fool me once, shame on you. Fool me twice, shame on me.*

I realise I've lost focus, so I slow my breathing before turning to Tabitha.

'So, what, you're just a dogsbody, are you, for the Alumni?' I say. 'I mean, you're obviously not important enough to be in charge, are you?' I raise my voice to cover the sound of the phone keys as Brianna dials the emergency number. 'I bet it's always *Do this! Do that!* I bet you just hate being ordered about all the time, don't you?'

Tabitha glares at me. 'Shut her up, can't you?' she says to her son, but he doesn't move.

I carry on, aware of Brianna whispering into the phone behind Tabitha. 'I mean, it must be hard for you, having to do all the fetching and carrying, having them boss you around *all* the time. I bet you're fed up with it, aren't you? I bet you think you should be bossing them around, don't you?'

She strides over and raises her hand, ready to smack me across the cheek. I've obviously touched a nerve – but have I given Brianna long enough to finish the call?

'Mum!' says Arthur in evident horror. 'She's fourteen, for goodness' sake!'

'I don't care,' she says. 'She and her friends are *not* going to mess up our plans now, not after all these years, when we're so close to being sworn in as full members—' She breaks off mid-sentence, and shrieks, 'Hang up that phone, *now*!'

Tabitha charges at Brianna, who stands fixed to the spot, looking terrified.

I shout, 'No!' but it makes no difference. I feel powerless as I watch the scene unfold.

Liam, who's closer, runs to block Tabitha's way, but he's too late. Brianna and the handset go flying in different directions.

And then our beloved friend is lying on the tiles,

her face pale and her eyes closed. Is she all right? Did she strike her head on the sideboard? I need to get over to her, but there are too many people between her and me.

'Brianna!' I shout, but there's no answer.

'Tie up the girl,' says Arthur's mother, nodding towards our unconscious friend.

Arthur is nearly as pale as Brianna. 'I don't think she needs restraining, Mum – she needs a doctor.'

'Nonsense. She's just unconscious. We need to make sure these three don't leave and go to the police.'

'You can't keep us prisoner,' says Liam.

She smiles at him. 'Of course we can,' she says cheerfully. 'I bet no one knows you're here, do they? If you'd actually managed to contact the police earlier, your friend wouldn't have been trying again just now, would she?'

My heart is beating too quickly. I close my eyes briefly and take a deep breath. As I open them, I slow my breathing right down, focusing on calming my thoughts and body.

It works. Now, with a clarity that Mr Zhang would

applaud, I can visualise what I have to do. If we're going to escape, we'll need to unlock the gate. I scan first Arthur and then his mother, and spot a bunch of keys, hanging from Tabitha's belt. Now all I need to do is get hold of them.

Arthur takes a length of rope from his back pocket (who carries rope in their *pocket*?) and sets about lifting Brianna into one of the armchairs and lashing her to it, while his mother looks on and gives unhelpful, contradictory instructions.

I ask loudly, 'Is Sheila still alive?'

Arthur stops for a moment. 'Of course she is,' he says. 'I told you – we aren't hurting anyone.'

'So who did?' I insist. 'And where is Sheila? What have you done with her?'

'*Arrrrgggghhhh!*' Tabitha's scream makes us all jump. She rounds on me. 'I have had enough of your pitiful little whiney questions. Tie her up with her boyfriend,' she tells her son.

Arthur shepherds Liam and me towards the armchairs. This is my moment – if I don't do something now, we're going to be captives, with little hope of rescue or release. I catch Liam's eye as we traipse dutifully along, and mouth, *'Duck on three . . .'*

He nods, and I mouth, 'One . . . two . . .'

As I shout *'Three!'* Liam crouches down, giving me access to Arthur. Using the heels of my palms, I strike Arthur in the sternum and navel simultaneously and he falls to the floor, landing on the tiles with an unpleasant crunch. I hope I haven't been too rough. There isn't time to worry about that, though – Tabitha's coming straight for me.

'Get Brianna!' I shout to Liam, who immediately runs to our friend's side and starts to untie her.

Tabitha is squaring up to me. She's taller than I am but very thin – she doesn't look strong. I hope I'm right. I close my eyes for a split second. When I open them, I see her fist coming straight for my face. But I'm fully focused. As her blow meets the palm of my hand, I continue the trajectory, sending her off balance so that I only have to get out of her way for her to fall.

She lands awkwardly but scrambles straight back up and comes for me again. This time, she lowers her head and charges towards my belly. Again, I wait for the optimal moment . . . As I step out of the way, she can't slow the momentum and ends up running into the wall. She crumples to the floor and lies still.

There's no time to waste, though – I can hear Arthur starting to groan. I dash to his mother's side and unclip the keyring from her belt before running over to Liam. 'Have you freed her?' I ask.

'Yeah. And she's coming round.'

'I feel sick,' mumbles Brianna. Liam and I put each put an arm round her waist and the three of us stagger out into the hall.

As I'm opening the front door, I hear Arthur saying, 'Mum? Mum! Are you all right?' but we carry on making our way outside.

'How are we going to get past the gate?' asks Liam. I dangle the set of keys in front of him. 'With these. I managed to snatch them from Tabitha's belt.' And with that, I lock the front door behind us, trapping Arthur and his mother inside the house.

We make it out of the park gates and lock them behind us. I drop the keys in a nearby bin. Hopefully, that will slow Arthur and Tabitha down a bit, if they do try to come after us.

'We'll have to take a cab,' I say, as we limp along. Brianna's far too weak for us to move quickly. She's taller than I am, and her weight bears down on me uncomfortably. The three of us are like a bizarre version of the three-legged race, with too many legs and not enough capable runners.

As soon as we're far enough away from the signal blocker, Liam orders a black cab through an app on his phone.

'It should be here any minute,' he says. 'It's just a street away.'

When the taxi pulls up, I call out to the driver and he gets out and comes over to help.

'What's happened to her?' he asks, helping us to set Brianna gently down on the back seat.

'She had a fall,' I say.

'So you need to go to the hospital?' he asks.

'No. My friend here is a trained first-aider, so

he's checked her over. We just need to get her home.'

The driver climbs into his seat and meets my eye in the rear-view mirror. 'Was she drinking?' he asks. 'This is very bad – she looks too young for to be drinking alcohol.'

Liam shakes his head. 'No – nothing like that. We were at a party, and someone was mucking around and took her chair away just as she went to sit down. She fell backwards on to some tiles.'

I'm impressed by my friend's quick thinking. It's such a plausible lie.

'Ouch!' says our driver. 'Where does she live?'

Liam catches my eye. 'Is it safe to go to hers?' he asks quietly.

'It's got to be better than my place,' I say. 'They know where I live.'

'Cadogan Place, please,' Liam tells the driver.

I close the connecting window and call Sofia Solokov.

She answers on the third ring. 'This had better be good, Agatha Oddlow, or you'll be in big trouble for waking me at one o'clock in the morning.'

'I'm sorry, Sofia, but I need your help.'

'Hold on – aren't you suspended?'

'Yes, but . . .'

'Let me guess, you've got the – what's the expression? – *the bit between your teeth* and you're not letting go?'

I sigh. 'Look – my friend Liam was able to trace the registration number of the car that kidnapped Arthur and me . . .'

'Oh, yeah – the professor told me you'd been abducted. Sounds pretty scary.'

'Yeah, it wasn't fun.'

'What do you need?' Her tone is resigned – as if we've been in this position a hundred times before, which seems a little unfair.

'I need you to send a team over to a house called The Lodge, which is at the entrance to Greenwich Park. That's where they'll find Arthur and his mother, Tabitha, who both need taking into custody. The Guild will also have to take possession of the five paintings that were delivered there tonight by helicopter. Now, I'm sure Arthur and Tabitha know where Sheila Smith is being held, so they'll need to be interrogated . . .'

'Stop! You're going too fast, Agatha. What are these paintings you're talking about?'

I quickly fill her in on the secret helicopter delivery.

'Wow,' she says, 'you really think those are stolen paintings?'

'I think it's more likely they're forgeries, waiting to be swapped with the originals.'

'So,' she says, 'what time do you think the drop was scheduled for?'

'The drop . . .?'

'If the forgeries have just been supplied, there must be a drop scheduled – a pre-arranged delivery to a person at their home or gallery.'

'So maybe instead of arresting the Fitzwilliams,' I say slowly, 'we should have them followed, to see who they're meeting.'

'Hmm, maybe,' she says. 'I'll talk to the professor – see what she wants to do.'

'But I'm worried about Sheila. I think we should

rescue her as soon as possible. I've found some evidence that suggests the Alumni killed my mum . . .'

'The Alumni?'

'Oh – that's the organisation Arthur's working for. They're obsessed with keeping masterpieces for people they reckon really appreciate art, or something.'

'And you think they had something to do with your mum's death?'

'I know they did – but I haven't got time to go into all that now.'

'You're right. I'm typing a message to Professor D'Oliveira . . . She should be receiving it . . . right now . . .' She pauses, then says, 'What about you?'

'What about me?'

'Now that the Fitzwilliams are on to you, it's important we keep you safe until we've caught them. Where are you planning on going now?'

'Cadogan Place – it's Brianna's house. I thought the three of us could stay there until the morning.'

'That sounds OK. I'll post a couple of plain-clothes guards outside, just to be on the safe side.'

'Thanks, Sofia.'

I picture Dad, on his own at home. What if the Alumni send someone over – perhaps that big man who they sent to intimidate Mr Cohen? A montage of images of Dad being threatened fills my mind, and my breathing becomes quick and shallow, my palms sweaty.

But, as if she can read my thoughts, Sofia says, 'Shall I also have a couple of people posted outside your house, until daylight, to keep an eye on your father?'

'Oh, would you? That would be brilliant – thanks so much, Sofia.'

'No worries. We can't have anyone getting hurt on our watch.'

We finish the call, and I text Dad to let him know where I am so he won't worry. Then I check on Brianna. She's a better colour and is sitting straighter, watching London go by through the window. Liam's removed his coat and she's wearing it draped over her like a blanket. She looks a lot younger than her age and it makes me feel protective – and guilty too, for dragging her into this.

'You OK?' I ask her, and she smiles and nods.

'I'm feeling much better. I could really do with some sleep, though. I keep nodding off.'

'We're nearly there,' says Liam.

Sure enough, at that moment we turn off Sloane Street and drive along another road for a minute before arriving at the far end of Cadogan Place. It's not long before the taxi is pulling up in front of Brianna's house.

'You're sure you'll be all right?' the cabbie asks, when we open the connecting window to pay him.

'We'll be fine,' says Liam. 'Our friend's much better already – look . . .' And Brianna manages a smile as she climbs out.

'Thanks so much for your help,' I say.

Two Guild agents are already in place opposite Brianna's house as we approach the front steps. One of them discreetly shows me the Gatekeepers' key logo – on a label inside his woolly hat – and they nod to me. I feel safer for knowing they're there.

Brianna is doing so much better that she's now able to climb the steps without Liam's or my support.

She unlocks her front door and we follow her in and turn on the hall light.

'Straight to bed,' says Brianna. We walk upstairs together to the first floor, where she points to a series of doors and says, 'Pick any of those.'

But I'm not happy about the idea of leaving her alone overnight, when she's just had a bad bang to the head.

'Can I share your room?' I ask. 'I'd like to be sure you're OK.'

'That's fine. I just have to sleep . . .'

The three of us end up all sleeping in her room – with Liam in her plush armchair, and Brianna and me sharing her enormous bed. If we hadn't all been exhausted from the night's adventures, we could have had quite a fun slumber party. There's always next time.

17.

CHOCOLATE CAKE
FOR BREAKFAST

'I can't believe we're out of the investigation,' I say. 'I mean, all these years I've wondered what happened to Mum, and now I've discovered the organisation who hurt her . . .'

Liam nods in sympathy.

He and I are sitting in Brianna's kitchen. She's still fast asleep upstairs and we don't want to disturb her. We've raided the fridge, but all we could find was a giant chocolate gateau, so we're eating slices of that for breakfast. It seems like Brianna's brother doesn't believe in stocking up on healthy food.

'I'm not going to that meeting with the professor,' I tell Liam as I lick the last traces of chocolate off my teaspoon.

He takes a sip from his mug of tea and raises an eyebrow. 'Why not?'

'She's bound to be busy with the Fitzwilliams and the forgery ring. In any case, she'll just give me more reasons why I'm banned from the case – and I've got more important things to do. I've got to find Sheila, and work out what happened to Mum!'

My mobile begins to ring.

'Who is it?' asks Liam.

'I'm not sure . . .' I answer the phone cautiously. 'Agatha speaking, hello?'

'Agatha – Elizabeth MacDonald here.'

'Oh, hello! I wanted to call you, but I've been taken off the investigation . . .'

'Yes, Professor D'Oliveira has told me. But I need to speak to you, face to face, if that's all right? It's about Arthur Fitzwilliam.'

'Of course.'

'How does nine o'clock sound? Too early?'

'No, that sounds fine,' I tell her. 'I'll see you then.'
We end the call and I message Sofia:

> Hi Sofia. Any news about the Fitzwilliams? Please tell the professor I won't make the 8.30 meeting. Dr MacD has asked me to meet her at the gallery at nine. But please don't tell the prof that

My phone pings almost immediately with a response from Sofia:

> Our little birds had flown the coop, so no joy

I hold my phone up so Liam can read it. 'Arthur and his mum weren't there? What happens now?' he asks.

'Hopefully, they won't have got far. At least now that the Guild know they're criminals, they'll be on the lookout for them.'

Liam hesitates. 'I'm not sure it's safe for you to go to the gallery, while they're at large, Aggie.'

'It's a public place. It's probably as safe as anywhere,' I say confidently. I get up from the table and wash my mug and plate, leaving them to drain on the side. 'Meanwhile, I need a wash and some clean clothes.'

Upstairs, Brianna is awake. She greets me with a big smile. 'You're still here! I was worried I'd have missed all the action.'

'There was plenty of action last night.'

'You know what I mean . . . What happens now?'

'I'm going to the National Gallery, to meet Elizabeth MacDonald, the director.'

'Ooh – can I come?'

'It's not going to be very interesting, to be honest. I don't think there's much point, sorry. Look . . . would it be OK if I had a shower and borrowed some clothes?'

'Of course. *Mia* wardrobe *es sua* wardrobe. Or something like that. You know what I mean: you can help yourself to anything you like.'

She hands me a clean towel and shows me into her en-suite bathroom, where I take a shower. It feels luxurious to stand under the hot stream of water after all the fighting and running.

I don't take too long, though, conscious that I need to be at the gallery quite soon. When I'm dry, I rummage through Brianna's 'closet' (actually a huge separate room). At another time, I reckon I could spend at least a couple of hours in here, but today I just need an outfit suitable for a business meeting. I pick out a dark-grey pleated skirt and a red sweater. With thick black tights and my DM boots, I reckon I'll pass.

While I'm dressing, it occurs to me that Mr Cohen might be a useful person to take to the meeting. He can take a look at *Sunflowers* to verify Arthur's findings with the XRF spectrometer.

Sitting on the edge of Brianna's bed while she goes for a shower, I dial the conservator's number. He answers quickly, still sounding on edge.

'Yes?'

'Mr Cohen? It's Agatha.'

'Oh, thank goodness you're all right! I've been worried about you – feeling that I should have talked you out of continuing.'

'I think you tried . . .'

'Was there something specific you wanted now?'

'I was wondering whether you could meet me at the National Gallery,' I say.

'What, now?'

'Not quite – but at nine? I've got a meeting with the gallery director.'

'With Elizabeth MacDonald? Why do you want me to attend as well?'

'I'm hoping you can check out the *Sunflowers* painting, to verify once and for all if it's genuine or a forgery. Also, I might need you to tell Dr MacDonald what you know – about the threats to my mum and to yourself. I don't want to make her panic about Sheila, but she needs to understand what the Alumni are like.'

'I see. Yes – I'm sure I can make that. I'd better leave straight away, though.'

'That's great – thank you.'

'See you at nine, Agatha.'

'See you then. Bye.'

Once clean, dry, dressed and booted, I go back

downstairs to find my friends. Liam's also wearing different clothes.

'Brianna's brother had some stuff I could borrow,' he says. He's in a navy cotton sweater and navy jeans, and looks classically, geekily handsome.

'Nice,' I say, and he blushes.

It's hard to tell if Brianna's changed her clothes or not. So much of her wardrobe tends to feature torn black jeans and black tops with holes in, that one outfit looks very much like another.

'Shall we head off then?' she asks.

I pull an apologetic face. 'Like I said, I'm not sure there's much point in the two of you coming along. And you did just get knocked out, Bri.'

Liam grabs his coat. 'We're not letting you go anywhere alone, Aggie. Not after that abduction.'

'What about school?' I ask.

He shrugs. 'What about school?'

'What – Liam Lau actually *choosing* to miss school? Am I being a bad influence on you?'

'Always. And I wouldn't have it any other way.'

We grin at each other, until Brianna coughs.

'Taxi?' she says, and we troop outside to flag one down.

Mr Cohen's already waiting outside the National Gallery when we arrive. He looks nervous and a little dishevelled, as if he's dressed in a hurry.

'Ms Oddlow!' he says, as I disembark.

'Hi, Mr Cohen. Thanks so much for coming. These are my friends, Liam Lau and Brianna Pike.'

He shakes their hands politely before we all make our way up to the entrance. There's a security guard on duty there. When I show him my ID badge, he nods and waves us through. 'Dr MacDonald's waiting for you in the Van Gogh exhibition,' he says.

I'm surprised – I'd expected her to want to meet me in her office, for the sake of privacy. But the gallery's not open to the public yet, I suppose.

As we walk up the stairs to the exhibition, Sam Cohen asks, 'Have you tracked down Sheila?'

I shake my head. 'Not exactly. But we have found some people who know where she is.'

'Is she all right?'

'I hope so.' I wish I could give him a more positive response. Arthur said the Alumni weren't hurting anybody, but that obviously wasn't the case with my mum.

We reach the entrance to the exhibition, and another staff member greets us. 'Oh, there are more of you than expected,' he says with a frown.

'These are my friends,' I say, gesturing to Liam and Brianna, 'and Mr Cohen's an art conservator.'

The guard nods and radios someone, presumably Dr MacDonald. 'I have Agatha Oddlow here, ma'am, with two friends and a Mr Cohen . . . Right . . . right . . . Yes, ma'am.' He nods to us. 'That will be fine. Please go on through.'

We traipse into the first room, where the sight of *Sunflowers* takes me back to the first time I met Arthur.

I've paused, mid-stride, and Liam has to touch me on the shoulder. 'Are you all right?'

I nod. 'Just thinking again about how naive I've been.'

'Hey – he's obviously highly trained in deception. Don't blame yourself.'

We move further into the room, and Dr MacDonald walks towards us. She's quite sprightly for a lady of . . . whatever age she is – quite old, anyway. She's still got the 'autumn of her years' as she put it ahead of her on her clan's precious island, so maybe her family all live to very old ages.

'Ms Oddlow, Mr Cohen – thank you for coming. And these are . . .?'

'Brianna Pike and Liam Lau,' I say.

She nods to them, then turns back to me. 'I was hoping, however, we might talk in private, through there,' she says, indicating the adjoining room.

'Of course,' I reply. 'In fact, Mr Cohen was just going to do a preliminary examination of some of these paintings.'

'What? Right now?'

I nod. 'We thought it might be helpful for you.'

'It would have been more helpful to have been notified in advance of your intentions.'

'I'm sorry,' I reply, feeling slightly surprised. 'I thought you'd be pleased.'

'Pleased to have an outsider come in to my gallery, to judge the authenticity of my collection?'

Sam Cohen steps forward. 'Of course I won't do anything, if you don't want me to, Dr MacDonald,' he says. 'I didn't realise you'd not been consulted . . .' He frowns at me.

'Why don't you three wait for me here?' I say quickly to defuse the situation. 'I'll go with Dr MacDonald through to the next room for a moment.'

The director and I walk past the empty attendant's chair to the room containing *The Yellow House* and *Bedroom in Arles*. And then I freeze. There may be no attendant, but there's someone waiting in the room: Tabitha.

I try to back out, but the security guard has followed us in, and blocks my way. Just as I open my mouth to shout for help, Dr MacDonald kicks me hard in the back of my legs and I lurch forward. The fall seems to last for several seconds, and the main emotion I register is surprise. Despite her authoritative manner, Elizabeth MacDonald had seemed so . . . harmless.

18.

IMPOSSIBLY FAMILIAR

Lying on the floor and momentarily winded, I run through the mistakes I've made. I normally pride myself on not making assumptions based on people's age or appearance – Professor D'Oliveira is elderly, quick-thinking and feisty, after all – but I've slipped up . . . MacDonald seemed so *proper*, in that old-fashioned kind of way.

As the man dressed as the security guard wraps rope round my wrists and ankles and knots it, I close my eyes and try to work out my next move. They can't get me out of here while Sam Cohen and my friends are in the next room. Unless – and this

thought is like a cold stone in the pit of my stomach –
other Alumni members have also been sent to attack
them. There's no sign of Arthur – what if he's using
his fighting skills on Liam and Brianna? They
wouldn't stand a chance. I fight back tears. Why didn't
I pass some of my fighting skills on to my friends?

I have to get us out of this, but how? I reassure
myself with the thought that I did tell Sofia I was
going to meet Dr MacDonald this morning, at the
gallery. Maybe the Guild will come looking for me . . .

The man drags me to my feet and shoves me
through to the first room, where I see three more
thugs, presumably all members of the Alumni,
restraining my friends. They look scared but as far
as I can tell they aren't hurt. However, unless the
Guild turn up soon, I can't envisage a positive
outcome here. Brianna, Liam, Sam Cohen and I have
all been captured because we know about the forgery
ring. Our knowledge is only going to end with . . .
I shudder, not wanting to finish that thought.

'Take them to the lifts,' says Dr MacDonald. I feel
a rough hand on my back, propelling me forward,

and I stumble along, my movement restricted by the ropes.

'Who are you working for?' I ask her, as we pass out of the exhibition.

'I'm not working *for* anyone,' she says. 'Everyone here is working for me.' She leads us through a staff-only door to the lift lobby.

'So you're the head of the Alumni?' I ask as she pushes the button to summon the lift.

'Aye. Someone needed to take control of the art world, before the ignorant masses inherited it all.'

'Oh, really? A generous motive indeed, I don't think!' I say angrily.

'What's taking so long?' tuts Dr MacDonald, pushing the button repeatedly, as if that will somehow encourage the lift to perform more efficiently. 'It's been on the roof level for far too long.'

'So who else is involved in this?' I ask her.

'You're every bit as tenacious as your headstrong mother, aren't you? Such a shame you were both on the wrong side.' She sighs again and turns towards me. 'The Alumni are a *secret* organisation,

Ms Oddlow – we do not expose the identity of our members.'

'And you don't make money out of this?'

From the shocked look on her face, you'd think I'd slapped her.

'We believe in preparing for a healthy and *comfortable* retirement, surrounded by exquisite works of art, such as mere members of the public could never truly appreciate. It's no loss to *them*. Believe me, after nearly fifty years as the director of a *public* gallery, I'm well placed to judge the unworthiness as far as art is concerned of most men and women.'

She turns back to the lift, which still hasn't begun its descent.

'Where are you taking us?' I ask her.

'Somewhere you can't communicate with your agency,' she says.

'Where is that, exactly?'

'Oh, tsk tsk. Can't you keep her quiet?' she asks the man who's restraining me.

'Not without a gag,' he replies.

'So gag her!'

'Please don't!' instructs a voice behind me. It's Liam. He, Brianna and Sam Cohen have arrived in the lobby, together with their captors. Even without the masks, I recognise the two Alumni members who kidnapped Arthur and me yesterday and held us captive in the barn. Sals catches my eye but at least she has the grace to look away immediately, as if she's ashamed.

'Leave it, Liam,' I say, desperate to keep my friends from harm for as long as I possibly can.

'This thing must be broken!' says the director in exasperation.

But, as soon as she's said it, the lift begins to descend. We watch the numbers light up slowly, one at a time. It feels a bit like a countdown to an execution. At least the man holding me seems to have forgotten about the gag. My legs are wobbly with adrenaline and fear, but I'm still looking for an opportunity to get us out of here.

Finally, the G for 'ground floor' is lit up and there's a ping as the lift arrives. The doors slide open and I see a woman cowering in the far corner of the metal box. As I my eyes adjust to what I'm seeing, I realise it's her – *Sheila!* – dishevelled but still recognisable from her photo—

There's a sudden loud thud close by, and one of the henchmen hits the ground hard. As he falls, he takes Dr MacDonald down with him. Then there's a confused silence before anyone thinks to retaliate against the invisible assailant. In that moment, Tabitha Fitzwilliam lets out a shriek and topples sideways, landing with one leg at an awkward angle.

And then I spot her, fighting her way through like an Amazonian warrior: a tall woman with a forest of brown hair. She must have come rolling out of the lift, slamming straight into the nearest henchman. Now she's spinning and kicking out at our bewildered captors, who don't seem to stand a chance.

The man who was holding me steps towards her, but she aims a jab at his jugular and simultaneously kicks his knees from under him. He makes a strange, gurgling noise as he falls.

The woman arrives at my side and I feel her loosen my ropes.

'Come on, Agatha,' she says. 'You need to act now.'

This is enough to nudge me into action. While I work with my new ally, using the moves Mr Zhang has taught me to disarm and unbalance my opponents, a confused sense of recognition is ringing in my head. This woman is not a stranger. I know her. I know her well.

But it's not possible . . . is it?

As we take down the final henchman, I say:

'Mum . . .?'

Our victim falls to the floor, where he lies groaning.

Then she turns to me, with tears in her eyes, and says, 'Yes, darling – it's me.'

My mum, Clara Oddlow, is standing in front of me, holding out her arms – as if she's expecting me to jump into them.

I stare at her, a tangle of possibilities racing through my mind. Could this be a lookalike or an impostor? But my instincts all tell me this really is her.

'I don't understand . . .' I say at last.

19.

THE SILVER SERPENT

Mum leads me to a bench in the main gallery, where we sit side by side. She tries to take my hand, but I snatch it back. I feel too . . . What do I feel? *Angry*, I realise – *furious*. And betrayed.

Around us, the Alumni are being rounded up and led away in handcuffs by Guild members, but none of that seems important any more.

We sit in silence, until Mum says, 'You've grown up so much since I last saw you. You were a very determined little girl, who knew lots of long words. And you had a great sense of justice, even then.'

I don't say anything. My head is whirling with

thoughts and questions. At last, I say, 'How's this possible? I thought you were dead. I don't understand!'

'I got too close to uncovering the identity of the top figures in the Alumni,' says Mum quietly. 'So they sent someone they knew I trusted. I thought he was taking me to confront them, but he transported me to a small cell on an island called Fairhaven . . .'

I start to sob. 'But surely you could have escaped before now?'

'I needed help to get out,' she says. 'I was kept in a cell with three locked doors, each with a different type of mechanism. I tried everything, Aggie – you must believe me . . .'

I shrug. 'It seems to me that a Guild agent as talented as *Clara Oddlow* could escape from anywhere – if she wanted to enough.' My voice sounds harsh and sarcastic.

'Aggie, look at me.' Grudgingly, I turn my eyes to hers, which are filled with tears, just like mine. 'Listen to me,' she says. 'I tried everything to get away.

340

Every day, all I thought about was you and your dad. I lay awake at night, imagining how my little girl would be wondering what had happened to me – why her mum had never returned. I hated the thought that you might believe I'd chosen to leave you. I never would do that.' She says this fiercely, with her fists clenched. It's then that I notice the scars on her fingers and knuckles. I take one of her hands and examine it.

'What are all these marks?' I ask.

'Oh!' She laughs. 'That's what happens to you when you try to break locks with only your wits and your bare hands.'

I look her in the eye again. 'You really did try to escape, didn't you?' I say quietly.

She nods gravely. 'I really did, Aggie, so many times . . .'

Something melts in me. I throw my arms round her and she hugs me back tightly.

'So how *did* you get free?' I ask eventually, when we finally loosen our hold on each other.

Mum takes a deep breath. 'There was a young man

who used to visit regularly, delivering packages, which I'm pretty sure contained paintings. He always checked I had enough food and drink. Sometimes, he even brought me books. He told me to call him the "Silver Serpent".' She laughs again. 'I think he fancied he was in a spy thriller or something. A few days ago, Sheila was brought to the island too and kept in prison with me. The young man was the one who helped us both escape.'

'That was Arthur,' I say. 'He was my partner in the Guild.'

She frowns. 'But that makes no sense. He was working for the Alumni.'

I shrug. 'He was a double agent.'

'Right . . .' She pauses for a moment, as if absorbing the new information, before continuing with her story. 'He seemed to do a lot of the running around and administrative stuff for the Alumni. Anyway, he used to turn up with that skinny, bossy woman we've just apprehended,' says Mum.

'Tabitha Fitzwilliam,' I say slowly.

'That's right! It was clear she was his mother

from the way she spoke to him. They were always arguing, but she usually won. He was obviously scared of her.'

'How did he free you?' I ask.

'He came on his own, late last night, with the helicopter. He spoke very little – just unlocked the cell and led Sheila and me out.' She pauses. 'Sheila was scared – she was worried he might be taking us away to kill us.'

'Weren't you afraid of that too?' I ask.

She shakes her head. 'No. He seemed far too calm . . . and relieved – *happy*, even – as if he'd finally managed to do the right thing.'

'About time,' I say dully.

'He claimed to be your friend – it was one of the few things he said.' She pauses, recalling his words. 'Hmm, that's right – he said, "Please tell Agatha I'm doing this for her."'

So after betraying me, he rescues Mum. It's hard to reconcile the two deeds.

'He knew *all along* that you were alive,' I say, 'but he let me go on thinking you were dead.'

'People make tough choices,' she says, 'especially when they have domineering parents.'

I can't stop staring at Mum. It seems impossible, but she's really here.

Liam and Brianna come over, wearing foil wraps, like marathon runners. The Guild's paramedics must have been treating them for shock.

'You OK, Aggie?' asks Liam.

'Yeah. How about you two?'

'We're fine,' says Brianna. 'Been in much worse situations.' She smiles and looks at my companion.

'Brianna and Liam –' I take a deep breath – 'meet my mum, Clara.'

Mum takes one arm from round my shoulders and holds out her hand, but my friends just stare at her.

'It's all right,' I tell them. 'I reacted pretty much the same way as you. But Mum was a prisoner, because of her investigations into the Alumni. She only just managed to get away, after years of trying. Arthur freed her, and Sheila Smith.'

Liam doesn't smile, but he does take Mum's hand

and shake it briefly. Brianna just nods to her and Mum nods back. I'm still reeling from her reappearance, and can't decide how I feel. One minute, I'm ecstatic. The next, I want to cry, or scream in anger that the Alumni kept her from me for half my life. I keep thinking: *All these years without her, when she was alive the whole time.*

Mum turns to meet my gaze. 'How's your dad?' she asks. Her expression is full of serious concern.

'He's muddling along. But he'll do a lot better now you're back,' I tell her.

A team of Guild members go past, escorting Elizabeth MacDonald and Tabitha Fitzwilliam, and behind them comes Professor D'Oliveira.

'Good work, Agatha,' she says, patting me on the back. Then she sees Mum and stops dead on the spot. 'But . . . You . . .'

I've never seen the professor lost for words before.

'Hello, Dorothy,' says Mum.

The professor stares at her, the same way I did.

'Sorry to shock you like this,' says Mum. 'I've been held captive by the Alumni.'

'I thought you were dead for all these years . . .' says the professor. 'I never stopped blaming myself . . .'

'It wasn't your fault.'

'If I'd kept closer tabs on your investigation . . .'

'It wasn't your fault,' Mum says again.

The professor nods, then snaps back into her usual brisk self and says, 'We can have a full debrief at some point. In the meantime, where's poor Sheila?'

Mum points to a chair close by, where Sheila is sitting quietly, wrapped in one of the foil blankets, and Professor D'Oliveira strides over to talk to her. Mr Cohen appears from somewhere, also wrapped in a foil sheet, and when Sheila sees him she gives a start.

'Sam? What are you doing here?'

'Hello, Sheila. It's so good to see you,' he says quietly. 'Lots of people have been worried sick about you, including me.'

He sits down next to her and takes her hand, and I'm relieved that he seems to be coping better than I'd expected.

I spot Sofia, busy in the background, directing Guild

people and herding Alumni members. She catches my eye and gives me a thumbs-up, and I smile at her.

My mind, however, is still racing – there's so much to process. Over and over again, I squeeze Mum's hand and she presses mine in return. She's really here. But that doesn't come close to making up for all the years she was stolen from me. And from Dad—

'Mum, we have to get home to Dad,' I say, suddenly desperate for him to know what's happened.

She just nods. Her face is grim and anxious.

'It'll be OK,' I tell her, although I really have no idea if that's true.

20.

AN UNEXPECTED VISITOR

I don't want to let go of Mum, so I hold her hand all the way home in the taxi. Liam and Brianna are coming with us. I know – we could have had a private family reunion, but Mum was concerned for Dad. She knew he would find it difficult if she just appeared home unannounced, so we've agreed that my friends will go in ahead of us and prepare him for the shock. Liam and Brianna run on ahead and we give them ten minutes before we follow. I keep glancing at my watch, but time has never moved so slowly.

At last, I say, 'We can go now,' and we start to head

along the path towards Groundskeeper's Cottage. But Mum's pace is slowing as we approach the front door. I glance at her in concern, and then I realise what the matter is: she's afraid.

'It's OK,' I say. 'He's going to be thrilled.' The truth is, I have no idea what Dad will be feeling right now.

The door opens before we reach it, and Dad appears in the doorway, shadows under his eyes and his hair a mess, as if he's been running his hands through it.

He stands looking at Mum. At last, he says, 'It's really you.' I can't tell anything from his tone.

'It's really me, Rufus,' she says quietly.

He starts to cry and I let go of Mum's hand and run to put my arms round him. He can barely stand, and he's too heavy and tall for me to support on my own, but my friends come to help me and we support him to a chair in the hallway, where he buries his face in his hands and sobs, his whole body wracked by emotion. I keep my arms round him, but I can't tell if he's even aware that I'm there.

'Dad,' I say, 'Dad, it's OK,' but he just shakes his head.

'Rufus,' says Mum quietly. She's come inside the house, and is standing watching him. 'I know it's a lot to take in . . .' I step away from Dad, to give them space. My friends are standing further down the hall, and I join them. Brianna puts an arm round my shoulders.

'Seven years, Clara,' Dad says, looking up at Mum, 'you let us believe you were dead.'

She takes his hand and says, 'I was a prisoner, Rufus. They kept me locked up.' Her voice sounds pleading.

His face turns fierce and he says, 'Did they hurt you?'

She shakes her head. 'They ignored me mostly. Just kept me fed and watered.'

I watch as my dad – my big, strong dad – says, 'I don't know what to feel. I don't know what I'm supposed to feel.' He sounds lost and helpless, like a child.

'I know,' says Mum softly. 'It's OK.' She puts her arms round him and holds him tight, while he sobs. It's horrible to see him like that. I want to comfort him, but I know only Mum can do that right now. After a few minutes, she turns to me and nods for me to join them. I walk over and she puts one arm round me and keeps the other round Dad. He's quieter now and calmer, and he looks up at me with a watery smile.

That's when I know it's going to be all right.

It's been nearly a week since the Great Gallery Showdown, as Brianna's named it. My friends have stayed away, giving us time to be a family again, but they're here now, in my sitting room. I can't stop gazing around, feeling so much love for these four people.

'Tell us about Arthur,' says Brianna to Mum. 'He was a pain in the neck when we went to his house. What was he like when you met him?'

'I used to see him regularly. I quite looked forward to his visits. It was his mother who was the difficult one. She needed to throw her weight around.' She looks at me. 'He obviously thinks highly of you, Agatha.'

'But he was still a traitor,' I say.

'Maybe he didn't want to be,' says Mum. 'From what I saw, his mother had a very forceful personality.'

'It was still his choice. I'm sure he could have refused to go along with her.'

'He did, in the end, by helping Sheila and me escape.' She pauses. 'It's a shame he'll still be going to prison.'

'I should hope so too,' says Liam, who's sitting on the arm of the sofa, next to me. 'He treated Agatha appallingly.'

'And don't forget he tied up Brianna, after Tabitha knocked her out,' I say.

'Although those knots were pretty loose,' admits Liam. 'I got them untied in seconds.'

'Will his sentence be lighter, because he freed you and Sheila?' Brianna asks Mum.

'It should be. I'm going to put in a good word for him. And he's only seventeen, so it will be a juvenile detention centre rather than an adult prison.'

I'm not ready to forgive Arthur, so I don't say anything.

'How about you and the Guild, Aggie? Have you been reinstated?' Brianna asks me.

I pull a face at her to be quiet. Dad still hasn't forgiven me for joining the organisation, or for keeping it secret from him.

He speaks up: 'Agatha is not allowed to partake in any clubs, societies or secret organisations without first discussing it with her mum and me,' he says firmly. 'She has put herself and you, her friends, at risk and is clearly not old enough to make sensible choices.'

'So how many of the paintings turned out to be fakes?' cuts in Liam. I smile at him, grateful to him for changing the subject.

'They're still being examined,' says Mum. 'It's going to be tricky – there could be many more that we don't even know about yet. In the Van Gogh exhibition, it turned out to be only *Sunflowers* and *The Yellow House*. Thanks to the three turning up at the Fitzwilliams' house, that last drop of fakes was seized, saving a number of very valuable pieces.'

'I feel sorry for Lord Rathbone and Sarah,' I say.

'I know,' says Mum. 'I mean, as public figures go, he's a bit pompous, but he wouldn't harm a fly.'

'I shouldn't have just accepted everything Arthur told me. If I'd known the assistant at Sir John Soane's Museum was his mother, I would never have believed what she told me about *The Marriage* – that Lord Rathbone had sent it for cleaning.'

'Ah, hindsight is a wonderful thing,' says Mum wryly. 'Don't beat yourself up over it, Aggie – Arthur was a skilled agent.'

'But I just accepted everything he said.'

'Of course you did,' says Liam. 'He was your partner.' I smile gratefully at my friend.

'At least Lord Rathbone wasn't charged with anything in the end,' says Brianna.

'Do you think his reputation's been damaged, though?' I ask.

Mum shakes her head. 'No, slurs slide off that man. He'll bounce right back.'

There's a knock at the door and we look round at each other in surprise – everyone's here already. I go to open it. There's an elderly woman on the doorstep, dressed in a pink coat with a matching hat.

'Professor D'Oliveira!' I say. 'Would you like to come in?'

'That would be very nice, Agatha. Thank you.'

I take her coat and show her through to the living room where the chatter subsides as soon as I open the door and the visitor makes her appearance.

Then Mum says, 'Dorothy – it's so lovely to see you!' She leaps up and gives the professor a kiss and her ex-boss pats her on the shoulder.

Dad gives up his seat, and the professor accepts, thanking him as she sits down, with a gracious nod like a queen. He goes to perch on the arm of Mum's chair.

'I still can't get over how little you've changed, Clara,' the professor says, smiling at Mum. 'Tell me – how did you keep so well, for all those years? Sheila Smith looked so drawn, after just a few days in captivity.'

Mum looks very sad for a moment. 'The hardest

part was the emotional and mental side,' she says. 'Physically, there was no real hardship. I exercised in my little cell every day, and set myself puzzles to solve to keep my brain active. What else can I say, Dorothy? I'm an agent. You trained me well. But, as I say, the hardest part was the emotional side. Nothing could have been worse than separating me from my loved ones for seven years.' She looks up at Dad and then over to me. 'The only thing that kept me going was promising myself I would get back to them – that one day I'd make it home.'

The professor just nods sadly. Then, after a pause, she turns to me. 'Arthur has proven to be a bit of a double, or triple, agent, hasn't he? But at least now we know who took your mother's file, Agatha.'

'Really?'

The professor nods. 'It was Arthur. I'm guessing that as soon as the Alumni found out you were joining the Guild, they knew you'd want to continue your mother's investigation into them.'

'That makes sense,' I say. 'It meant I had to find out about Mum's investigation from her hidden notes instead. The Alumni wanted to stop me making the link between the forgeries and Sheila's disappearance much sooner.'

'Ah, so they had more than one motive for getting their hands on the file,' says the professor. She clears her throat. 'Speaking of motives, I have one of my own for this visit. I'm sure it's all right to speak in front of Agatha's friends . . . I just wanted to ask you if you would be coming back, Clara.'

Mum looks startled. 'To the Gatekeepers?'

'That's right.'

I look quickly at Dad. He's stopped smiling.

But Mum doesn't even pause before replying, 'Not in a million years. I've lost far too much time as it is. I missed seeing my little girl grow up. Nothing can give me those years back, but I'm not missing anything else.' She smiles at me.

'Well, if you do change your mind, we'd be delighted to have you back—'

'Clara's just got home,' Dad breaks in, 'after seven years stuck in a cell on a remote island! Can't we just enjoy being a family again?'

Mum leans in to his chest and he puts an arm round her.

The professor nods. 'You're quite right, both of you. I didn't mean to be insensitive.'

'I was thinking that I might like to be a librarian,' says Mum.

'I see,' says the professor. 'It does seem a shame, though, to waste your skills.'

'I think Mum would make a great librarian,' I say.

'Thank you, darling,' she says, smiling at me.

The professor nods. 'I have no doubt that Clara Oddlow will shine at whatever she chooses to do.'

'Thank you, Dorothy,' says Mum, and she smiles at the professor warmly.

'Well, I'm starving,' I announce. 'Shall I make us all dinner?'

'I'd better let you all get on,' says the professor, easing herself to the edge of her chair, ready to get up.

'You're not going anywhere, Dorothy,' says Mum. 'I'm going to make us all a nice risotto.' She gets up and heads for the kitchen.

'I'll help,' says Dad, following her out of the room.

'They look like they're going to be all right,' says Brianna.

The professor nods. 'Give it time. There are a lot of emotions to be worked through, but I never saw two people who loved each other more than Rufus and Clara.'

I want to go through to the kitchen too, but I fight the urge. This is a constant struggle since Mum's return – knowing my parents need time together, but not wanting to let Mum out of my sight.

'She's quite safe now,' says Liam, as if reading my thoughts, 'especially as she has all of us to protect her,' and the professor and Brianna both nod reassuringly.

They're right. And now that I've got all my family together, including my closest friends, I'm going to take very good care that no one threatens any of us ever again.

ACKNOWLEDGEMENTS

Tibor Jones Studio is a boutique writing collective dedicated to starting aspiring writers' careers. We work under the name of Lena Jones, the fictional niece of the fictional Tibor Jones.

We would like to thank the following people for their help:

Martyn Morrisson of Phoenix Freestyle Kung Fu, for sharing his kung fu expertise; Adam in the library at Sir John Soane's Museum for advice about the museum's panelled display of paintings; Cleo Broda for introducing us to Anni Albers's typewriter artwork; and Mr Robinson, physics teacher at Plume Academy, Maldon, for explaining why it's impossible to travel at the speed of light, and so stopping us from inserting an erroneous passage!

The beautiful and super chic girl in Year Four at Corpus Christi who cut her hair in a bob and wore a red beret like Agatha on World Book Day this year; clever clogs Isaac Chesser, aged ten, and his family, who buy copies of Agatha Oddly for all their friends and family, and debate over their dinner if Agatha would ever wear hoop earrings while on an investigation; and Charlotte Colwill for her brave, creative navigation of book three.

We're especially grateful to Rosie Sanders – a talented writer and poet who has carried the Agatha baton with great aplomb. And the biggest thanks to her family, Andrew, Robert and Thomas Erskine, who shared their talented mother with us while this book was being written. You guys are the real stars of this show. Thomas and Robert are especially useful with ciphers and science – that's a fact.